Two Princesses

V.F. Odoevsky

Translated by Neil Cornwell

Hesperus Classics

Hesperus Classics
Published by Hesperus Press Limited
4 Rickett Street, London SW6 1RU
www.hesperuspress.com

First published as *Kniazhna Mimi* in 1834 and *Kniazhna Zizi* in 1839
First published by Hesperus Press Limited, 2010

Designed and typeset by Fraser Muggeridge studio
Printed in Jordan by Al-Khayyam Printing Press

ISBN: 978-1-84391-138-8

CONTENTS

FOREWORD

Princess Mimi is a monster, a *grande dame* with horny hands and greying hair, who has suffered the greatest calamity that can befall a Russian woman of high society in the 1830s: she has been left on the shelf without a husband. Her revenge on a younger generation of still eligible Russian beauties is to tease out their secrets and weave a web of poisonous rumours, so that she can then pass damning judgement on them all. Such scandal-mongering can lead to fatal consequences. But what do Princess Mimi and her crabby fellow guardians of social morality care, as they whisper behind their fans at the card table, waiting for another hand of whist?

Princess Zizi (short for Zinaida) is an altogether more worthy female heroine. Self-educated and determined, she has spent a frustrated and secluded girlhood attending to a domineering and selfish mother. Her imagination fed by sentimental novels and romantic poetry, she inevitably falls prey to the tangled passions of her own heart, burning with secret love for the first young man she gets to know – the attentive suitor who looks after her mother's financial affairs and ends up marrying her sister. Her unenviable fate is to keep house for the two of them and even care for their baby – a vicarious, humiliating shadow-marriage – until one day she is handed unexpected evidence of a plot to defraud the family and abandons all decorum to secure her rights.

The two Russian Princesses, protagonists of Prince Vladimir Fyodorovich Odoevsky's two society tales of 1834 and 1839, might at first glance seem to represent fairy-story opposites – the vindictive and the virtuous, bad and good. In fact they make good literary companions, the stories complement each other. And these two spirited, unfortunate women are not as unalike as you might think. We are privy to their initial girlish hopes, trace their disappointments, and watch their options narrow as opportunities slip away. We are encouraged to pose the question: What made them what they are? And what led them to act in such different ways?

There may be no nineteenth-century Russian equivalent of Jane Austen or George Eliot to illuminate the subtle internal workings of the Slavic female heart and mind. But from Pushkin's captivating heroine Tatyana in *Eugene Onegin*, and the sad Princess Mary in Lermontov's *A Hero of Our Time*, to the most complex and conflicted female protagonist of them all, Tolstoy's Anna in *Anna Karenina*, you can trace a chain of intriguing Russian literary heroines, all of them somehow trapped between what they yearn for and what society demands. And in this tradition, Odoevsky's two princesses also deserve a niche.

Princess Mimi's sharp-eyed, sanctimonious meddling is an exercise in self-preservation, a way to empower herself in a world where spinsters have little value. Others may fear and despise her, but at least her opinion counts. Scandal is her currency. The more of it she can generate and exploit, the greater her social worth. And she is not entirely deluded. Behind her rigid *froideur* in public lies hidden a desperately miserable woman who knows she has chosen to make herself unlovable, and faces the sharp tongue of her elderly mother and younger widowed sister at home.

'You are long past thirty, Mimi – for God's sake get married...' says her mother.

'It is my view... that much of all this is really your own fault,' says her sister. And she pushes the point home: 'Why do you have that incessantly scornful expression on your face...? You drive just about anyone away...'

Princess Mimi is not merely perpetrator, we realise. She is also victim. And it is the two-faced frivolous society into which she was born, Odoevsky tells us, which is most at fault.

'Do not lay the blame on her for all this, but blame, lament and curse the depraved morals of our society,' says his narrator. 'What is to be done, if the only goal in life for a young woman in society is marriage!'

For her part Princess Zizi is also caged behind the steel bars of early nineteenth-century etiquette (similar but surely far more rigid that the social rules Jane Austen's British heroines had to navigate). Indeed, of the two Princesses, in many ways Princess Zizi's initial situation is worse.

Princess Mimi may be consumed with bitterness, but at least she can look back on a lost love that was requited – a betrothed who wanted her and a marriage that nearly took place. It was only halted when at the last minute it emerged that the two of them were too closely related, for propriety's sake – a disaster which sent the bride-to-be into an emotional breakdown from which she almost died.

Princess Zizi, on the other hand, lives with the double agony of an ardour that she must both endure and bury on a daily basis – generated by and hidden from the brother-in-law whose household she devotes herself to running. And what is worse, when she does finally allow her secret to come to light, she confronts another far more terrible deception which makes her look a fool.

But unlike Mimi, Zinaida has something to fall back on: her private love of books and learning which, she confides to a friend, 'insusceptibly broadened my range of thought'. True, too much heady romance and sentimentality is no doubt what tipped her headlong into an ill-considered infatuation in the first place. We learn that she has read most of Richardson's

Clarissa, and is well versed in the poetry of Byron and the Russian Romantic poets. But she has also ploughed through history books and journals. So when she realises that she and her family are victims of trickery and her life is on the verge of being turned upside down, she does not collapse into hysterics. Pale and calm, she takes matters into her own hands, sets about hiring lawyers and throws social respectability to the winds.

Not surprisingly given the era and social circumstances into which she was born, Princess Zizi pays a price for showing such enterprise. She is shunned by society as 'odd', too clever and 'over-proud'. Afraid to show her face, she takes to appearing in public only at masked balls.

But as she grows older, her unconventional behaviour becomes less strange and more alluring to a younger generation in a Russia which is rapidly industrialising and changing fast. One such admirer is the businessman who tells us her story, a man over twenty years her junior, one of a 'new breed of fashionable industrialists'. The fact that she draws the belated appreciation of a man young enough to be her son illuminates Princess Zizi's tragedy: her education and independence of spirit made her a woman ahead of her time.

It takes only a cursory look at the biography of Prince V. F. Odoevsky to realise he too was ahead of his time. A creature of encyclopaedic interests, he was a music critic, philosopher, librarian and amateur scientist, as well as an avid educationalist, writing numerous stories for children and primers for the uneducated. Literacy and learning for women, one of the themes so intertwined in these two society tales, must have been a subject close to his heart.

His other stories range from Hoffmannesque Gothic fantasy to utopian philosophical musings and even an unfinished futuristic tale set in the year 4338 which can only be categorised as science fiction. It allowed him scope to imagine all manner of unfamiliar (elasticated glass, ladies' hats adorned with electric sparks...) and familiar inventions, from air travel to space flight and even a daily bulletin delivered directly into every home which sounds wonderfully like a twenty-first century internet blog.

So perhaps it is not surprising that this imaginative enlightened proselytiser of learning should have been so determined to highlight the shortcomings of contemporary Russian society by probing into its psychological impact on women.

There is one further poignant note of social criticism here that is worth sparing a thought for.

Prince Odoevsky was not only an observer of social mores. He was himself a pillar of Russian high society, a man whose frustrations at the pitfalls and pettiness of its prejudices were honed at first hand. Not only was he a popular writer in his own right, he hosted literary salons in St Petersburg and Moscow that brought together many of the best known Russian writers of the time.

'Our most warm hearted and unforgettable Prince Odoevsky,' says the writer Ivan Turgenev of him in his *Literary Reminiscences*, 'everyone remembers his handsome features, his mysterious and affable look, his childishly charming laughter and his good humoured solemnity.'*

True to that characterisation, Odoevsky for the most part does not preach to us but instead draws us in. Gentle irony, juxtaposition of narrative forms that offer contrasting points of view and vivid characterisation act as the prompts to allow us to make up our own minds. But he leaves little doubt there is

* David Magarshack, Faber and Faber, London 1959, p. 98.

one lamentable and pointless consequence of society's game which he believes has got out of hand.

In Russia in the 1830s duels were common fare of fiction and fact alike. And in *Princess Mimi* this is the ultimate barbarity which malicious misinformation can lead to. Two young men challenge each other to a duel. Their quarrel is based on ill-founded rumour, a misunderstanding which they luckily clarify in time. But even so, their inflated sense of honour means they cannot bring themselves to back down. Within minutes one of them is dead.

In Odoevsky's story this turn of events comes abruptly, a clumsy twist for which we somehow feel unprepared. But in a duel, of course, this is exactly what happens. One minute both stand facing each other. The next minute one man is dead.

Dismay at the meaningless waste of young human life through duels was not uncommon in Russia when this story was published in 1834. But in retrospect it must have cut close to the bone. Only three years after its publication Odoevsky's friend and arguably Russia's greatest ever poet, Alexander Pushkin, was killed at the age of thirty-seven in just such a duel, based on a quarrel over his honour and the reputation of his wife.

– Bridget Kendall, 2010

INTRODUCTION

Vladimir Odoevsky, his other careers and multiple activities apart (see our Biographical note), can be said to have enjoyed three almost discrete literary careers. The first comprised his youthful, formative and almost completely – if in at least some cases undeservedly – forgotten writings of the first half of the 1820s; this was interrupted by the consequences of the Decembrist uprising of 14th December 1825. The third saw a late return to writing, albeit in a minor key, after he had returned to Moscow, as a senior public servant, in the 1860s. By far the most important one, though, was that of his St Petersburg interlude, stretching, as far as its writing years were concerned, from the late 1820s until the publication of his three-volumed *Works* in 1844 (*Sochineniia*), from which he omitted virtually the whole body of his early period work. In this decade and a half he wrote almost all of the works for which he is now remembered, not to mention his engagement on a number of further ambitious and unfinished projects.

Odoevsky's work of the 1830s contains much with a society-tale setting, including the frame-tale elements of both his completed cycles, *Variegated Tales* (1833) and his much better known magnum opus, *Russian Nights* (1844). Such a setting can embrace either the familiar high-society social world (*bol'shoi svet*: of which, coming from his own princely lineage, he had abundant experience), or a more restricted depiction of the idealistic intelligentsia (often of the 1820s). In addition, many of his more Gothic or fantastic stories are set in the contemporary, or near-contemporary, *haut monde*.

Odoevsky's society tales of this period are in many ways a continuation of the main trends of his early fiction of the 1820s. The tone is frequently 'instructional', the setting is predominantly the salon or boudoir and the ballroom, and the subject matter is society intrigue (or 'drawing-room secrets'). Under scrutiny are the mores of aristocratic society and such associated factors – becoming by now increasingly prominent – as 'the woman question' (*zhenskii vopros*).

The present volume presents, here aligned as a pair, Odoevsky's two major contributions to the budding society tale – in the form of the long short story, or novella. This is the genre known in Russian as the *povest'*, or, for this high social-world sub-generic category of 'the society tale', the *svetskaia povest'* – itself a term which has been dated back to a review published in exactly this period (in 1835).

Princess Mimi (*Kniazhna Mimi*, published in 1834) is Odoevsky's most outspoken attack on the destructive, hypocritical and sterile aspects of *le beau monde* of Russian high society. It is, however, also worth consideration for its compositional quirks: the interposing of the digressive authorial 'Preface' about two thirds of the way through the story; and the (in fact highly relevant and generally underappreciated) comments on the anomalous state of the Russian language in high society, vis-à-vis salon French. An obvious artistic weakness may be said to be the hasty and melodramatic denouement, largely summarised in an abrupt conclusion. The main interest, however, lies in the relatively sophisticated attempt at the psychological portraiture of the vicious eponymous protagonist, Mimi, and in the treatment of the woman question.

Odoevsky may seem open to criticism, especially with more recent hindsight, for investing one of his more elaborate characterisations in an unambiguously negative female figure. However, the elevation of such a character to a position of central prominence was in itself unusual at this early stage in the development of Russian fiction. Furthermore, he may properly be justified for emphasising the role played by certain ladies as, in effect, guardians of male hegemony in the policing of female purity for patriarchal benefit. In any event, his overall attitude to the position of women (balanced, arguably, to a substantial extent by the figure of Princess Zizi in the second tale presented here) appears less hostile, or indifferent, than that of many writers of his epoch.

Odoevsky's attitude to the situation women face in society is perhaps not so very far from that adopted later by Tolstoy (while sparing us the latter's negative obsession with sexuality). There is criticism of the system of arranged marriage and of marriage in general as the only objective for women to be encouraged by society. Those who miss out, like Mimi, may understandably turn bitter and may then enjoy unlimited leisure in which to set themselves up as venomous arbiters of the morals of their social class. Mimi 'could become a good wife and a good mother of a family', we are told, 'or she could develop in the way that now she has.' In any case, and even at best, 'the wives had a voice and power in accord with their husbands.'

Odoevsky's concern with female education, observable in a number of his works, would appear to demonstrate that he, perhaps unusually progressively for a male writer of the 1830s in Russia, favoured a more positive alternative. His second important society tale of the 1830s, *Princess Zizi* (*Kniazhna Zizi*) was written in 1836, just in time to gain the approval of Pushkin for likely publication in his journal *The Contemporary*, but in fact published only in 1839 in the journal *Notes of the Fatherland*. In this work. In this work, more convoluted plot-wise than its earlier sister-tale) and again experimental in terms of narrative presentation, Odoevsky provides a variant depiction of the unmarried woman.

Princess Zizi (short for Zinaida) retains her integrity and wins through against the odds, taking on the legal system as well as her swindling and lecherous brother-in-law (who, however, it may be said, is also dispatched at a crucial moment – on this occasion through the agency of unruly horses – or an *equus ex machina*). She has, in the meantime, resisted an illicit passion for said brother-in-law, while remaining unscathed in the household to carry out her family duties to her hopelessly unaware sister and baby niece. In the words of one commentator (Sally Dalton-Brown), 'Zizi encapsulates the paradox of the society tale heroine who exists at the nexus of two forces, infernal emotion and chastity.'

Princess Zizi, who is on a number of occasions referred to as being 'strange', or having 'some very strange qualities in her character', may be seen as Odoevsky's attempt to present an emerging new type of 'strange woman'. Zizi is one who is allowed to remain in a relatively triumphant and almost envied form of spinsterhood, still attracting the attentions of would-be admirers. While such a portrayal might appear less than an ideal of liberation, certainly from more recent perspectives, it is at least striking for its period. The work is littered with literary references and clichés, furnishing it with a strong veneer of romantic pastiche. Nevertheless, Odoevsky's consistent stress over a number of works on 'the woman question' as a strong part of his social, or societal, critique can be seen as justifying overall the impression that a serious element does here underlie his generally tongue-in-cheek compositional approach.

Odoevsky's contribution to the society tale and its input into mainstream nineteenth-century Russian fiction is not to be underestimated. Richard Peace, indeed, takes *Princess Mimi* 'to be almost the quintessence of the society tale'. His society tales and settings, taken together as a body of work, contain a considerable store of detail on Russian society of the first four decades of the nineteenth century. Many of them employ a retrospective chronology, stretching back over a number of years, with the occasional hint that 'now' things might have changed, at least just slightly. An element of ambiguity or uncertainty is accentuated throughout by the employment of irony, eccentric modes of narration, schematic characterisation, aphorisms, travesty, pastiche and other devices commonly found in European and Russian romantic prose.

The most immediate influence, say of *Princess Mimi*, was marked in the prose works of Lermontov, especially in his unfinished novel *Princess Ligovskaia*, written in 1836 (the forerunner to the exploits of Pechorin in the redoubtable classic, *A Hero of Our Time*). Another aristocratic writer, (Count) V.A. Sollogub, produced his emblematic contribution to the sub-genre, entitled indeed *High Society* (*Bol'shoi svet*) in 1841 (the year that saw the second edition of *A Hero of Our Time*). However, one should also look much further ahead; it is to be hoped now with better-informed social insight, to scenes and characters in the mature and larger-scale works of Russian fiction by Goncharov and Turgenev, Dostoevsky and Tolstoy. *Anna Karenina*, for instance, whatever else it may be, can certainly be seen as a prime example of the society tale writ large.

– Neil Cornwell, 2010

Note on the Introduction

Material for this Introduction has been re-worked from my contributions to the volume *The Society Tale in Russian Literature: from Odoevskii to Tolstoi*, edited by Neil Cornwell (Rodopi: Amsterdam and Atlanta, GA, 1998), which developed from a symposium on the society tale held at the University of Bristol in 1996. Quotations from S. Dalton-Brown and Richard Peace are taken from their essays in the same volume.

See also:
Joe Andrew, 'V.F. Odoevsky and the Two Princesses', in his *Narrative and Desire in Russian Literature, 1822–49* (Macmillan: Basingstoke and London, 1993, pp. 50–84)

And, for further reading:
Neil Cornwell, *The Life, Times and Milieu of V.F. Odoyevsky, 1804–1869* (London, 1986)
Neil Cornwell, *Vladimir Odoevsky and Romantic Poetics: Collected Essays* (Providence and Oxford, 1998)
Vladimir Odoevsky, The Salamander and other Gothic Stories, translated by Neil Cornwell, (London, 1992)
V.F. Odoevsky, *Russian Nights*, translated by Olga Koshansky Olienikov and Ralph E. Matlaw (reprinted Evanston, 1997)
Slobodan Sucur, Poe, *Odoyevsky and Purloined Letters: Questions of Theory and Period Style Analysis* (Frankfurt am Main, 2001)
Claire Whitehead, *The Fantastic in France and Russia in the Nineteenth Century: In Pursuit of Hesitation,* 'Legenda' (Leeds, 2006)

Princess Mimi

'Excuse me,' said the painter, 'if my colours are pale:
they're the best you can get in our town.'

Biography of a painter

1
THE BALL

La femme de César ne doit pas être soupçonée.[1]

'Tell me, who were you dancing with just now?' said Princess Mimi, stopping a certain lady with her arm who, having just concluded the mazurka, was walking past the Princess.

'Oh, he served with my brother once! I've forgotten his name,' replied Baroness Dauerthal as she passed and, tired out, she hurried back to her seat.

This brief conversation, unnoticeable to those around, twinkled fleetingly amid the general commotion that normally occurs following the end of a dance.

But this conversation made the Baroness start thinking – and not without reason. The Baroness, although already married for the second time, was still young and attractive; her kind personality, her sumptuous figure, her chestnut silky curls drew a crowd of young gentlemen to her. Each one of them couldn't help comparing Eliza to her husband, the husky old Baron, and to each of them, it seemed, her languid moisture-filled eyes communicated hope: only one experienced observer found in those dark blue eyes not the flame of voluptuousness but simply that southern idleness which, in his opinion, so strangely combines with northern phlegmatism in our ladies and goes to form their distinguishing character.

The Baroness was well aware of all her supremacies. She knew that, for everyone, her position beside the Baron appeared an impossibility, an affront to decency, some sort of absurdity. She knew too that at the time of her wedding the talk of the town was that she was marrying the Baron out of financial calculation. She liked never to leave the floor at balls, never not to have time to be pensive at receptions, always to have several fellow riders for a cavalcade; but she never permitted herself as much as a glance that could have indicated a preference for any one man over another – neither of delight, nor of pleasure, nor of distress: in sum, nothing of the sort that could set the soul in motion. Besides, from a sense of duty or from some sort of unnatural love for her husband, wanting to prove that she had not married him calculatedly, or simply the remark made by the above-mentioned observer being correct, or indeed from a combination of all these things – anyway, the Baroness was just as true to the Baron as was her little pet Beauty to her. She went out nowhere without her husband, even asking for his advice on what to wear. The Baron, for his part, had no doubts about Eliza's affection for him, allowed her to do as she liked and would just devote himself to his favourite pursuits: taking his snuff of a morning, a game of whist of an evening, and in between fussing around to procure himself yet further decorations.

Respectable society ladies had long been trying to track down an object for the Baroness' delicacy; but, whenever they gathered together at a summit to resolve the question, one would name some young gent, another would name another, and a third would suggest a third, and then the whole business would lapse into argument. To no avail they would run through all of society's eligible young men. No sooner had they agreed on one, either he would suddenly get married, or start running after some other lady – total despair would be the outcome! In the end, such unceasing failure just bored these guardians of morality. They decided that the Baroness was just wasting away time from their observation of other ladies. Unanimously, they found that the Baroness' art in the preservation of external propriety was worthy of the best morality, that she should stand as an example to other women, and so they set aside the matter of the Baroness, at least until any overwhelming circumstances should present themselves.

The Baroness was aware that Princess Mimi was a part of this moral estate, and knew also that this estate, for its part, would belong to that fearsome society that has got its tentacles into each and every social class. I'll open up a great secret; just listen!

Everything that gets done in the social world gets done for the benefit of this particular society without a name! It is the theatrical stalls; the other people tread the boards. It keeps its hands on authors, musicians, beautiful ladies, geniuses and heroes. It fears nothing – neither the law, nor truth, nor conscience. It passes judgement on life and death and its sentences are never changed, even should they be offensive to reason. The members of this society you may easily recognise in accordance with the following signs: other people play cards, but they observe the game; other people get married, but they attend the wedding; others write books, but they do the criticising; others give dinners, but they give the verdict on the cook; others do the fighting, but they read the military communiqués; others do the dancing, but they take up position close to the dancers. The members of this society recognise each other anywhere straight away, not by any special signs but by some sort of instinct; each one, before even listening properly to the matter in question, will already be in support of his or her confederate. Any of these members who might think of doing *something* in this world will be immediately stripped of all privileges linked to their calling, thus entering into the general stream of the accused, and with no means of regaining their rights. It is well known too that the most vital role in this law court is played by those beings for whose existence in this world it is absolutely impossible to come up with any justification.

Princess Mimi was the very soul of this society, and what now follows relates how this came about. You have to be told that she was never a really great beauty, though in her younger days she was not bad to look at. At that time she had no particularly defined character. You will be aware of the kind of feeling and the kind of thinking which can develop through the upbringing that women receive: a bit of design craft, something from a dancing teacher, a touch of slyness, *tenez-vous droite*[2] they get told, plus two or three stories from their grandmother as a dependable manual through this life and the next – that is just about their entire education.

Everything depended on the circumstances greeting Mimi upon her introduction into the social world: she could become a good wife and a good mother of a family, or she could develop in the way that now she has. In her day she did have her suitors; but the whole procedure just could not be handled. The first one, she herself just did not take to; the next was not of high enough rank and did not appeal to her mother; the third would have pleased both very much, and their betrothal took place with a wedding date announced – but the day before, to their surprise, they discovered that he was closely related, so the whole thing collapsed. Mimi was taken ill from the sorrow and very nearly died; however, recover she did. For a long time after that, suitors did not appear; ten years went by, and then ten more; Mimi grew plain and she aged, but to reject any idea of marriage, for her, would be terrible. How could she? To give up on the objective that her mother had pressed over and over again at family meetings; that her grandmother had kept on and on to her about on her deathbed? How could she renounce the idea that was the favourite topic of conversation with her lady friends, the one with which she had so long woken up and gone to sleep? This was really awful! And Princess Mimi carried on with her social life – ever with fresh plans in her head, but with sorrow in her heart.

Her situation had become unendurable. Everyone in her circle had already married, or was getting married; the little flirt who yesterday was seeking her protection was now herself already speaking in the tones of a protectress, and this was not to be wondered at – she had got married! This one had a husband covered in stars and ribbons! The husband of another one was a great whist player! Respect for the husbands got transferred to their wives; the wives had a voice and power in accord with their husbands; only Princess Mimi remained on her own, without any such voice or prop. Often at a ball she did not know who to latch on to, to the married girls or the unmarried girls or the married ladies, and this was not to be wondered at – Mimi was not married! The hostess would greet her with chilly courtesy, looking her over as she would an unwanted piece of furniture, and had no idea what to say to her, because Mimi was not getting married. And now and then there would be congratulations, though not for her, but always for some young lady who was getting married! Just a quiet whisper, unnoticeable smiles and overt or imagined gibes would fall upon the poor young lady who was possessed of insufficient skill, or excessive nobility, to sell herself into any calculated marriage!

The poor young woman! Each day her self-esteem suffered abuse; with each day came fresh disparagement; and – the poor girl! – with each day annoyance, malice, envy and vindictiveness, little by little, were despoiling her heart. Finally, her vessel overflowed. Mimi realised that, if not through marriage, then through other means, it was essential to maintain oneself in the social world, to give oneself some sort of value, to take up some sort of place. And so insidiousness – that dark, shy, gradual insidiousness, which makes society detestable and little by little whittles away its foundations – this social insidiousness grew in Princess Mimi to complete perfection. There developed within her a certain form of occupation: all her smaller aptitudes received particular direction; even her disadvantageous situation was turned to her advantage. What else was to be done? She had to maintain herself! And so Princess Mimi, as an unmarried woman, began worming her way into the company of single girls and the younger ladies; and now, as a ripe unmarried lady, she made herself an amiable companion in the serious debates of the older respectable ladies. And it was time she did! Having spent twenty years in futile expectation of a fiancé, she was hardly thinking of domestic worries. Dominated by a single thought, she built up in herself an innate loathing for printed type, for art, for everything known as feeling in this life, and applied herself totally to the malicious, envious observation of other people. She grew to know and to comprehend everything that was going on in front of her, and behind her; she made herself the supreme umpire over eligible bachelors and fiancées; she got into the way of commenting on every elevation in post or rank; she set up her own patrons and alumni, or protégés; she started lurking around where she could see that she was in the way; she began paying careful attention when talk was in a whisper; and, finally, she started talking of the universal depravity of morals. What else was to be done! She had to maintain herself in the social world.

And she achieved her aim: her humble, but unceasing and ant-like assiduousness to her business, or one should say to the business of others, accorded her real power in the drawing rooms; a lot of people were afraid of her and attempted not to fall out with her. Only naïve younger girls and youths would dare to laugh at her withering beauty, at her knitted eyebrows, at her heated homilies against the present era, and at her annoying behaviour, which had been turned into a habit, of coming to a ball and being driven home without having joined in even so much as a waltz.

The Baroness knew all about Princess Mimi's power and her dreadful court of law. Though – untarnished, innocent, cool and self-assured as she was – she was not afraid of persecution from it: until now the very circumstances of her life aided her in avoiding it; but just at this time the Baroness was in a highly embarrassing position. Granitsky, with whom she had just danced, was a handsome and stately young man with thick, dark side-whiskers; he had spent almost the whole of his life in other countries, where he had become friendly with the Baroness' brother. The Baroness' brother was now residing in her house and Granitsky was a guest of her brother, as he knew almost no one in town. Every day he would have dinner and go out and about with them. In short, everything was drawing him closer to the Baroness and she was quite aware of what a fine romance a virtuous soul can construct on such an opportune foundation. This thought was occupying her while she was dancing with the young man and she was unwittingly searching her mind for a means of keeping at bay the backbiting of virtuous ladies. The Baroness, with annoyance, recalled that Princess Mimi's abrupt question, so closely matching her own train of thought, had thrown her into a state of confusion which, no doubt, had not been hidden from the piercing gaze of the spy-mistress. It had already seemed to her that there had been something particular in the Princess' voice in asking this question; moreover, she had noticed that straight away the Princess had begun talking with some ardour to an older lady sitting beside her, and that they were both, as though reluctantly, first smiling, and then shrugging their shoulders. All this rushed through the Baroness' head at a single moment, and at that same moment an idea was born – to get two things done at once: to avert suspicion from herself while gaining the Princess' favour. The Baroness began to look round for Granitsky, but didn't find him. And for that there was a reason, indeed a very important one.

At the far end of the house was to be found a secret room to which men were not admitted. A huge mirror there, brightly lit up, reflected the curtains of blue silk; around this was to be found every whim then in the quaintest of fashion: flowers, ribbons, feathers, locks of hair, mittens, rouge – all thrown about on tables, just like in the arabesques of Raphael. On a low divan there lay in rows blue and white shoes from Paris – this as a reminder of pretty little feet which seemed bored and solitary. At a little distance, under a light coverlet and piled over the back of an easy chair, were those enigmatic fabrications of civilisation which the wise woman will not display even to that person most entitled to her full candour: all those elastic corsets, lace garments, suspenders, those unintelligible starched kerchiefs hitched up on to a fancy cord or tied half way along, and all the rest of it. Only Monsieur Ravi, with his splendid crest of hair as though cast in porcelain, in his white apron with clippers in his hands, had the right to be in this ladies' sanctum when a ball was on.

The magnetic atmosphere of this female toiletry, from which a tremor would run through the body of any other man, had no effect on Monsieur Ravi. He took no notice of these sumptuous impressions remaining in the female attire, so well understood by the sculptors of antiquity who would moisten Aphrodite's veil. Like the superior of a sultan's harem, he would placidly doze amid all that surrounded him, without a thought as to the meaning of his name, or to what a room like that might suggest to a more fiery fellow countryman.

Just before the end of the mazurka, a certain young lady, uttering a couple of words to her gentleman partner, unnoticed by the others, flitted into this room, showed Monsieur Ravi her untwisted ringlet, and Monsieur Ravi went out to get his other curling irons. Instantly the young lady ripped a piece of paper down from its pad, quickly took out a slim pencil from her pocketbook, leaned her little foot on the divan and wrote a few words, rested against her knee; she compressed her note into an imperceptible ball and, when Monsieur Ravi came back in, she protested at his slowness.

After the end of the dance, when a number of unfinished utterances are hanging in the air, restless male dancers bustle from corner to corner after the ladies, ladies look down their list for the contradance in leisurely fashion, and even the stationary figures standing around those dancing change their places so as to display some semblance of life – just at this time of confusion, that same lady walked past Granitsky. A smoke-coloured scarf flew from her inflamed shoulders, Granitsky lifted it, the lady leaned forward, their hands touched, and the rolled-up scrap was left in the young man's hand. Granitsky's face did not change; he stayed for a little while where he stood, thoroughly straightened the glove on his hand and then, uttering complaints about stuffiness and fatigue, walked off at a quiet pace to a distant room where a number of players were seated in pleasant seclusion at a card table. Fortunately, one of them informed Granitsky that his stake had been lost. Granitsky moved to the side, pulled out his wallet and, as though searching in it for money, read these words, hurriedly scribbled by a hand he knew:

'I had no time to forewarn you. Don't dance more than once with me. I think my husband is beginning to notice...'

The rest was indecipherable.

By right of the indiscretion conferred on storytellers, we shall declare by whom this note had been written. Granitsky had known the writer of it when she was still a young girl: she had been his first love; back then they had exchanged vows of eternal love, but various family reckonings had stood against any such consummation – this had been in Florence. They soon parted; Granitsky set off for Rome. His Lydia was taken off by her mother to Petersburg and, like it or not, given in marriage to Count Rifeysky. However that may be, having met again, the lovers of old remembered their earlier vow: their fire blazed up from under the ashes. They decided to retrieve lost time and, in order to get their own back on the social world for its wilful behaviour, to rejoice in deceiving it.

Granitsky delivered to the Count a whole box full of recommendation letters, presents, packages and so on. He succeeded in performing some sort of service for his benefit in that very Petersburg, and eventually made himself almost a family member in his household.

Obeying the mistress of his spirit, returning to the hall, he started looking around to see whether there might be there ladies he knew, who might assist him in bringing his evening to a conclusion. At that very minute, the Baroness approached him and asked him whether he would like to meet a lady with whom to dance. Granitsky accepted her suggestion with great pleasure; and she took him up to Princess Mimi.

But the Baroness had made a miscalculation. The Princess went red in the face, answered that she was feeling unwell, and declared that she had no intention of dancing; and, when the Baroness had retreated in confusion, sounded off to the older lady seated beside her:

'Why ever did she suppose she could palm her friends off on me? She must be wanting to use me as a cover for wiles of her own. And she thought I wouldn't guess what she was up to...'

An entire world of spite came into these few words. How the Princess would have liked someone to come up to her now with an invitation to dance! How pleased she would have been to have shown the Baroness that it was just her Granitsky with whom she didn't feel like dancing! But this, unfortunately for the Princess, did not happen; and through the entire ball she, as was usually the case, did not get up from her chair, and she travelled home with plans for a most severe vengeance.

You should not think, however, my dear readers, male and female, that the Princess' malice towards the Baroness had occurred only from a momentary annoyance. Oh, no! Princess Mimi was a very sensible woman and had long schooled herself not to go too far without due reason, just from some heartfelt impulse. No! Long, long ago Eliza had given grave offence to Princess Mimi. In the final period of her cavortings about the ballrooms, Eliza's first husband had seemed something like a quasi-suitor of the Princess – that is to say, he did not have towards her the same aversion that other men had. The Princess was convinced that, but for Eliza, she would now have the delights of being a married woman, or, at very least, a widow – which would produce no less a pleasure. But all this was in vain! The Baroness had appeared on the scene, made off with this admirer, got herself married to him, tired him to death, got married to someone else – and was still liked by everyone, still aroused men's passions, and was able never to leave the ballroom floor, while Princess Mimi was still unmarried, still a spinster, and time was running on and on! Often over her toilette, the Princess would look in clandestine despair at her own charms, now past their prime: she would compare her lofty build, her width in the shoulders and her masculine air with the Baroness' small and well-moulded visage.

Oh, if anyone could have spied into what was then developing in the Princess' heart! What her inspiration was dimly conjuring! How resourceful all this was at such a moment! What a fine model she could have made for an artist wanting to paint a wild island-woman torturing a captive who had chanced into her lot! And all this had to be confined beneath a tight corset, beneath conventional phrases, under a courteous exterior! The blaze of an entire inferno could be let loose only as the thinnest imperceptible thread! Oh, it is ghastly, ghastly!

In these minutes of sadness, sorrow, envy and anger, a bringer of consolation presented herself to the Princess.

This was the Princess' maid. The maid's sister had been taken on by the Baroness, the sisters would often meet and, having had a proper go about their respective mistresses, would start disclosing to each other their household happenings. Then, having returned home, they would communicate all the news they had collected to their good ladies. The Baroness would die with laughter hearing the details of Mimi's toilette: how she had to suffer, tightening her rather wide waist; how her horny hands, gone blue from the strain, she then had to whiten; how she would add by various means to her slightly bent-in right side; how to her purple cheeks she would attach for the night – and what a horror! – raw cutlets;

and how she would pull unwanted hairs from her eyebrows, tinting the grey ones, and so on.

The news now received by the Princess was far more significant. And this was the Baroness' own responsibility: there was almost nothing to say about her, and Masha – as the Princess' servant was called – willy-nilly had to fall back on making things up. That ancient saying, proven through experience, does have truth on its side: people will always be the cause of their own misfortune!

When the Princess had got back from the ball, although this was a time when she would always be in a bad mood, on this occasion Masha noticed that something in particular must have occurred with her mistress. It seemed to her that there was some immediate shuffling about with shoes, jars of pomade, glass items and other things which, in such circumstances, the Princess had a tendency to send (to send – how to say this more delicately?), to send in a certain trajectory that parallels the floor and follows a height terminating with the maid's face. That seems to be obscurely enough stated... The poor girl, so as to stave off this storm cloud, could not fail to resort to her one means of defence.

'I was at my sister's today, ma'am,' she said. 'Oh, what things there are going on there, your highness!'

Masha was not mistaken. In a single instant the Princess' face cleared; she immediately paid the fullest attention and, long after the city noise had got started, Masha was still holding forth to the Princess about how the Baron often went away, how at this time a *new arrival* would be sitting with the Baroness, and how they would be agreeing to go together to the theatre, to be together at the ball, and so on and so forth.

It was ages before the Princess could get to sleep and, even when she did get to sleep, she was incessantly woken by a series of dreams: first she seemed to be getting married, standing in front of the lectern with everyone congratulating her – when the Baroness suddenly appears and drags off her fiancé. Then the Princess is examining her wedding gown, trying it for size and admiring it – when the Baroness appears and pulls the dress to pieces. Then the Princess is lying in bed, with a desire to embrace her husband – but it is the Baroness who is lying in the bed and laughing. Then the Princess is dancing at a ball, with everyone enraptured by her beauty and talking about her dancing with her fiancé – when the Baroness sticks out a leg and the Princess topples to the floor. But there were also dreams of greater consolation: the Baroness appeared to her as a maid – the Princess curses at her, hits her with shoes and cuts away at her hair all round. Then she appears in the form of a big black poodle – the Princess orders it to be chased out and she looks out of the window in delight as the lackeys pelt her enemy with stones. Then she came again as a design-canvas – the Princess stabs this with a big sharp needle and embroiders it with red stitches.

Though do not lay the blame on her for all this, but blame, lament and curse the depraved morals of our society. What is to be done, if the only aim in life for a young woman in society is marriage! – if, from the cradle, these words are heard, 'when you get married!' She is taught to dance, to draw, and music – in order that she should get herself married. They dress her up, cart her out into society and make her pray to the blessed Lord, just to get married more quickly. This is the end and the beginning of her life. That actually is her life. What a surprise, then, if every woman turns into her personal enemy, and if the first quality sought in a man should be worthiness of worship. Lament and curse, do! – but don't curse the poor young lady.

2
THE ROUND TABLE

'On cause, on rit, on est heureux.'[3]

Romans français

Under cover of silence and tranquillity, in
one's family circle…

Russian novels

The next day, after dinner, Princess Mimi, her younger sister Maria – a young widow – and the old Princess, the mother of them both, along with a couple of other family members, were sitting as usual at the round table in the drawing room and, while awaiting their partners for whist, they assiduously occupied themselves with their craft-design work.

The old Princess was a very elderly and venerable lady. Over the whole of her long, long life it would not be possible to find a single action, a single word, a single sense which had not been utterly thought through in accordance with received decorum. She spoke French very soundly and correctly; she fully retained the severity and the inaccessibility seemly to a woman of high social tone. She had little taste for abstract argument, but for whole days she could carry on conversations about this and that; she would never take upon herself the disagreeable responsibility of siding with someone at variance with received opinion. You could be sure not to encounter in her house any person who would be looked upon askance, or whom you would not encounter in society. What is more, the old Princess was a woman of unusual cleverness. She was a woman of no great wealth, able to give neither dinners nor balls; but she nevertheless could expertly dive into intrigue, expertly cordon people off with the aid of all her nephews, nieces, grandsons and granddaughters, so expertly ask after one person and tick off another that she gained widespread respect and, as the saying goes, had got herself on to a firm footing.

What is more, she was a very philanthropic woman. Despite her position of insufficiency, her drawing room was illuminated each day and officials from foreign embassies could be confident of always finding at her house an open fire, or a card table behind which time could be passed between dinner and some ball. In her house, raffles in aid of the poor would often be held; she was always overloaded with concert tickets emanating from the teachers of her daughters; she would patronise anyone, provided there was a recommendation from some respectable person. In short, the Princess was in all respects a decent, prudent and philanthropic lady.

All this, as we have said, accorded her a right to widespread respect: the Princess was aware of her value and was fond of utilising her due. However, for some while now, everything had started to seem tedious and annoying to the Princess. Whist and people, people and whist, still to an extent revived her, but before the beginning of the game she could not (just within the family circle, of course) hide her unwitting anguish, and some sort of cruel-heartedness would suddenly surface, some sort of petty detestation for everything around, a sort of lack of any amiability, a sort of aversion towards performing any kind of service – some sort of aversion, even towards life. And how was she not to bemoan her lot? Why should there be such unfairness? Why should this venerable lady have been so ill rewarded? For, I can assure you, this mini-Byronism of the Princess' sprang not from the remembrance of any kind of previously hidden sins, not from any repentance – oh, no, certainly not out of repentance! I have told you already that throughout all of her life the Princess never permitted herself to do anything at all that others would not have done: she had the innocence of a dove; she could boldly survey the happenings of her earlier life – they were as pure as a glass, clean as a whistle, not the slightest little stain. In short, I cannot in any way account for the cause of the Princess' anguish. Let this enigma be resolved by those venerable ladies who may, or may not, read me, and let them make sense from it to their grandchildren, to the hope of the new generation.

And thus the old Princess, in the middle of her family, was sitting at the round table. Oh, family round table! Witness to so many household secrets! What have you not had confided to you? What is there that you don't know? If your four legs were augmented with a head, you would be comparable even with our most serious scribes of social morality, who so truly and keenly come down on a society incomprehensible to them, and whom I attempt so vainly to imitate.

At the round table, things usually start with modest candour; a touch of spite, compressed from some other occasion, expands a little at a time; and selfishness leaps from beneath the design-canvas in its full and sumptuous flower. At this point, the steward's accounts and the derangement of the estate get a mention. Then the insuperable desire to get married, or give away in marriage, is brought out into the open. Now some failure or other, some moment of disparagement, is recalled. Next there will be complaints directed at very dearest friends and at people to whom one would appear wholly devoted. Then daughters start murmuring, the mother gets angry, sisters accuse each other. In short, here is where are made clear all those petty secrets which are so painstakingly hidden from the gaze of the social world. The ring of a bell is heard and it all disappears! Selfishness is concealed behind dark-coloured lace-ups, a smile will appear on the face, and the eligible bachelor coming into the room will look, moved with emotion, upon the so friendly circle of a loveable family.

'I really don't know,' the old Princess had been saying to Princess Mimi, 'why you bother going out to balls, when every time you complain of finding it boring… of not dancing… Outings cost money, and it's all to no end! It's just for me to stay at home alone, without even any whist… Just as I did yesterday! It really is time all this should come to a conclusion: you know you are long past thirty, Mimi – for God's sake get married, and make haste about it! At least I would then be able to calm down. I'm really not in a position to go on keeping you in dresses…'

'It is my view,' said the young widow, 'that much of all this is really your own fault. Why do you have that incessantly scornful expression on your face? Whenever someone comes up to you, from your face anyone would think it was a personal insult. You really are dreadful when you are at a ball… you drive just about anyone away from you.'

Princess Mimi. 'Should I really be hanging round the neck of anyone I meet, the way your Baroness does? Should I show off with affectations of gratitude to every silly boy for offering me the honour of being led into the contradance?'

Maria. 'Don't speak to me about the Baroness! Your conduct towards her yesterday at the ball was such that, I really don't know how to put it! Well, it was an unparalleled incivility. The Baroness wanted to do something pleasant for you, so she brought a gentleman over to dance with you…'

Mimi. 'She brought him over to me, using me as a cover for her own amorous ruses. That's doing me a wondrous favour!'

Maria. 'You always love seeing a bad side in everything. Where do you get these amorous ruses from?'

Mimi. 'And you are the only one who sees and hears nothing! You, it goes without saying, having been a married woman, may well hold the opinions of society in contempt, but I – I have too much self-regard. I don't want to start being talked about in the same way as your Baroness.'

Maria. 'Really! What they've said about the Baroness so far has all turned out to be not true…'

Mimi. 'Of course, everyone else is wrong! Only you are right! … I cannot admire sufficiently the way you can still take her part. Her reputation is quite established.'

Maria. 'Oh, I know! The Baroness has plenty of enemies, and there are reasons for that: she's very attractive; her husband is a monstrosity; her kind manner draws a crowd of men over to her.'

Mimi blazed up and the old Princess cut Maria short,

'To tell you the truth, I am not a bit pleased with your acquaintanceship with the Baroness; she has no idea at all how to conduct herself. What are all these endless cavalcades and picnicking? And there isn't a ball at which she hasn't done the rounds; not a man with whom she doesn't relate like a brother. I don't know what all this is called by you nowadays, but in our day such behaviour was called improper.'

'But we're not concerned with the Baroness!' retorted Maria, who wanted to divert the discussion from her friend. 'I am speaking about you, Mimi: you truly do make me despair. You talk about social opinion. You really don't think that it's on your side, do you? Oh, you're really quite wrong! Do you think it's nice for me to see that your tongue frightens people stiff, that they just shut up when you go up to some circle or other? They speak to me, to me, your sister, of your tittle-tattling, of your malevolence. You drop hints about his wife's secrets; you tell a wife things about her husband; the younger people just can't stand you. There isn't a piece of mischief that you wouldn't have known about and wouldn't have laid down the law on. I can assure you that, with your disposition, you will never ever get married.'

'Oh, that really doesn't bother me overmuch!' Mimi replied. 'I would rather spend a lifetime of spinsterhood than get married to some diseased cripple or other, and wear him out to death around the ballrooms.'

Maria, in her turn, had blazed up in anger and was just getting her answer ready, when the bell rang, the door opened, and in came Count Skvirsky – a very old friend or, much the same thing, a very old card partner of the old Princess'. He was one of those lucky fellows whom one cannot but envy. For a whole age and a day he had been fully occupied: of a morning he would have to congratulate so and so on their nameday, then buy a pattern for Princess Zizi, look out a dog for Princess Bibi, call in at the ministry to get news, catch up with a christening party or a funeral, and then make off to dinner, and so on, and so on. Over the last fifty years, Count Skvirsky had kept intending to achieve something in the way of serious business, but he kept postponing this day after day and, due to his perpetual involvements, had not even had time to get married. For him, it was all the same whether it was yesterday or thirty years ago: fashions and furnishings may have changed, but drawing rooms and cards remained the same things. Today like yesterday, and tomorrow like today – by now he was already revealing to a third generation his immutable and placid smile.

'It makes one's heart happy,' said Skvirsky to the old Princess, 'coming into the room to you and looking at your tender family circle. Today there are no longer many such concordant families! All of you together, always so jolly, so contented – and one gives an unworthy sigh at the recollection of one's own single quarters. I can give you my word of honour – and others can say what they like – but to the best of my concern, what I think anyway, is that a single life…'

Skvirsky's philosophical disquisition was cut short by the handing to him of a playing card.

Meanwhile the Princess' drawing room had swiftly filled up. Here would come: married couples whose own home is not much better than a Kalmyk wagon, fit just for an overnight stay; and those so cherished younger people who pop into your at-home just so as to have something to talk about at their next port of call; and those whom fate, flying in the face of nature, has sucked into the drawing room flywheel; plus those for whom the most routine visit is a result of the deepest reckoning and will be a resource for year-long intrigue. There were also such people as for whom even Griboedov[4] would be unable to come up with any more characteristic a name than Mr N. or Master D.

'Did you stay very long at yesterday's ball?' asked Princess Mimi of one young man.

'We were still doing some dancing after supper.'

'Tell me, then, in what way did the *commèdia* end?'

'Well, Princess Bibi did finally manage to get her comb to fasten…'

'No! That's not…'

'Ah, I see what you mean! That tall figure in the black frock-coat eventually took it upon himself to get into conversation; he brushed his hat against Countess Rifeyskaya and said, "Oh, I do apologise".'

'Oh, that's not it, either… Therefore, you didn't notice anything?'

'Oh, are you talking about the Baroness?'

'Oh no! I wasn't even thinking about her… But why did you start to speak about her? Is there really something they are saying?'

'No, I haven't heard a thing. I was just trying to conjecture what you were meaning by your question.'

'I wasn't meaning anything.'

'But what is this *commèdia* you mentioned?'

'I was just speaking generally about yesterday's ball.'

'No, have it as you please, there is something behind all this! You adopted such a tone…'

'Well, that's the social world! You are already deducing inferences! I assure you I had no one particularly in mind. But apropos the Baroness: did she dance a lot after I had gone?'

'She never left the floor.'

'She isn't looking after herself at all. With her health…'

'Oh, Princess! It's not her health you're really talking about. Now I understand it all. It's that Guards Colonel…? Isn't that it?'

'No! I didn't take any note of him.'

'So, if you will allow me? I have to recollect everyone she danced with…'

'Oh, for goodness' sake, that's enough! I tell you that I was not even thinking about her. I so dread all this tale-telling and scandal-mongering… People are so spiteful in society…'

'Allow me, allow me! Prince Piotr… Bobo… Leidenminz… Granitsky…?

'Who's he? That newcomer, the tall fellow with dark side-whiskers?'

'Exactly.'

'He seems to be a friend of the Baroness' brother-in-law, doesn't he?'

'Exactly.'

'So, he's called Granitsky?'

'Do please tell me,' said one lady who was seated at cards, listening keenly to Mimi's words, 'what exactly is this Granitsky?'

'Oh, the Baroness turns up with him everywhere,' replied a neighbour of the Princess' at the ball.

'And today,' put in a third lady, 'she was showing him off in her *loge*.'

'Only the Baroness could think that one up,' said the Princess' neighbour. 'God only knows what or who he is! Some sort of a visitor from the other world...'

'But really, though, he is God knows what! He is some type of a supposed Jacobin, or if not exactly a Jacobin then *un frondeur*, who doesn't know the way to live. And the rubbish he talks! Recently, I was just starting to urge Count Boris to get a ticket for our Celini, when this – what's he called, Granitsky or something? – began running on, right beside me, about a sort of insurance office that's being set up to do with concert tickets...'

'He is not a good man,' a number of people remarked.

'The Baroness had better not hear you saying that!' said Mimi.

'Ah, I understand now!' a young man interrupted.

'Oh, no! Really and truly, I only meant in the sense that this conversation would be disagreeable for her; he being a friend of their household... And for all...'

'Please allow me to interrupt you once again, since I can tell you exactly what you wanted to know. The Baroness, after supper, never stopped dancing with Granitsky. Oh, now I can see the whole thing! He never left her: she leaves her scarf on a chair, he will fetch it over; or she feels a bit hot, so he tears over with a glass...'

'How wicked you are being! I wasn't asking you about anything of that sort. It's little wonder that he should be taking good care of her! He is almost one of her own, he does live in their house...'

'Ah! So he lives in their house! There's quite a bit of self-confidence about that Baron! ... Isn't that right?'

'Oh, for goodness' sake, that's enough! You are making me come out with things that I'm not even thinking: with you it's straight into scandal-mongering – and I really do dread all that! Lord, preserve me from passing remarks about anyone! And especially about the Baroness, whom I do so love...'

'Yes! She is deserving of love, and... of pity.'

'Pity?'

'Without a doubt! You must agree that the Baron and the Baroness *together* do make a strange couple.'

'Yes! That is true! ... The Baroness' husband doesn't devote himself to her in the slightest: she's just at home, the poor thing, always on her own...'

'Not on her own!' the young man retorted, smiling at his own smart-wittedness.

'Oh, you turn everything round in your own way! The Baroness is a perfectly virtuous woman.'

'Oh, let's be fair, now!' the Princess' neighbour remarked. 'There's no need to censure anyone; but I am at a loss as to what principles the Baroness has. I don't know, but discussion somehow got on to *Antony*,[5] to that horrible, immoral play. I couldn't sit through it to the end, but she suddenly started standing up for that play and was trying to tell us that only a play like that could restrain a woman on the brink of perdition...'

'Oh, I must admit,' remarked the old Princess, 'as for all that's being said, done or written in the present period... I understand absolutely nothing!'

'Yes!' replied Skvirsky. 'I will tell you that, as far as I am concerned, what I think is that we must have morality, but that enlightenment is also...'

'Now it's you, with the same thing, Count!' the Princess retorted. 'Nowadays, everyone goes on about "enlightenment, enlightenment!" – whichever way you turn, it's enlightenment all over the place. The merchants are being enlightened, the peasants are being enlightened – we didn't have this in the old times, and everything went more smoothly than it does now. I pass my judgement in the time-honoured way: what they say is enlightenment, but take a good look – and it's debauchery!'

'No, do allow me, Princess!' replied Skvirsky. 'I am not in agreement with you. Enlightenment is imperative, and I'll demonstrate this to you, just like twice two makes four. So, what is enlightenment then? For example, there's my nephew. He passed through the university with all his scholarship: mathematics and Latin – he has his degree certificate and all career roads are open to him. He can be a Collegiate Assessor or go into the other services. So, allow me to say it: there is enlightenment, and there is another enlightenment. For example, take the candle: it gives light, and we couldn't play our whist without it, but were I to take the candle and bring it up to the curtain, the curtain would catch fire...'

'Allow me to note that down!' said one of the card players.

'What I have just been saying?' asked Skvirsky, with a smile.

'No, the rubber!'

'You did a revoke, Count! How can you have done that?' said Skvirsky's partner with some annoyance.

'What? ... I did? ... Revoke? Oh, my goodness! ... Did I really? Well, that's what enlightenment does for you! ... Revoke! Ah, my goodness me, a revoke! Yes, indeed, it was a revoke!'

At this point it was impossible to hear anything that was said: they all started talking about Skvirsky's *faux pas* and all arguments, everyone's interests and sensitivities focused on that topic. Profiting from this general confusion, two of the guests imperceptibly slipped out of the room: one of them, seemingly, had only just arrived in town to get his bearings there, while the other was taking him round the drawing rooms to make introductions. On the face of the one could be seen annoyance and mockery; the other was quietly and carefully peering at the steps of the staircase they were descending.

'I have been fated from birth to keep meeting that idle so and so!' said the first. 'That Skvirsky is an old familiar – I used to know him in Kazan, and what he didn't get up to there! And here he is, still at his orations! And what about? About morals. And more remarkable than anything is that he is actually convinced of what he is saying. Just remind him that he brought absolute ruin on his nephews, whose guardian he was, and then he'll be in a position to ask – how does that stand in relation to morality? You tell me, please, how can you all possibly receive into society such an immoral person?'

His friend shrugged his shoulders.

'What am I supposed to do with you, my dear chap!' he replied, seating himself in the carriage. 'If you don't know our language, just learn it, learn it, old chap: there's no other way. What we have done here is to change around the significance of all our words, and to such a degree that, if you call someone immoral who wins at cards, slanders someone close to him, grabs hold of someone else's estate, no one will catch your meaning, and your use of that adjective will seem just odd. But if you give full vent to your heart and mind, hold out your hand to some victim of the social world's prejudices, or you try just to keep your door closed to any social reprobate, you will then straight away get called an immoral person – and then that word will be intelligible to everyone.'

After a short silence, the first one resumed,

'Do you know that, for me, your brilliant, grand receptions are far more tolerable! There, at least, people don't say much, they all have an orderly appearance, like real people: but God, spare me their family circles! Their moments of homespun candour are dreadful, just revolting – revolting even to the extent of being curious. The old Princess, as a judge of literature! Count Skvirsky as a defender of enlightenment! Truly, it's enough to make you wish you were an ignoramus.'

'Nevertheless, there was still some justice in what the old Princess was saying. You must see this yourself – what is there in present-day literature? Endless descriptions of torment, villainy, depravity; endless crimes, and yet more crimes…'

'Pardon me!' replied his friend, 'but the people who say that are those who haven't read a thing apart from some of the works of present-day literature. You take it as a matter of course, don't you, that it is damaging society's morality? As if there were anything left to damage, my dear chap! From the mid-eighteenth century on, everything has been so meticulously damaged that now, by our century, nothing remains to be damaged. And is present-day literature the only thing we can blame for that sin? For any one genuinely immoral present-day work, I can point out to you ten from the eighteenth, the seventeenth, or even from the sixteenth century. Now nakedness is to be found rather in words; then it was really there, in the actual imagination. You've only got to read Brantôme,[6] or even Tredyakovsky's go at *Voyage to the Isle of Love*.[7] I don't know anything in Russian that's more immoral than that book: it's a manual for the most shameful of coquettes. Now they don't write a book like that, for the sake of sensual delights.

Nowadays an author, in the teeth of the time-honoured rule "*si vis me pleurer*"[8] will blaspheme and just laugh away, so as to get the reader sobbing. All present-day literary nakedness is the last reflection of the authenticity of the past, the forced confession of the old transgressions of humanity, the tail of an ancient wayward comet, according to which – do you know what? – according to which you can judge that the very comet is moving away over the horizon, for whoever is writing doesn't sense it any more. And finally, present-day literature, it is my opinion, is a punishment sent down from above on to the ice-cold society of our day: not for it, with its hypocrisy, the gentle delights of poetry! It is unworthy of those! And it could be that it's even a salutary punishment – so inscrutable are the determinations of the human mind! It could be that this powerful means is necessary for our age; it may be that this continual shaking away at its nerves will arouse its dormant conscience, just as physical suffering can arouse a drowning man.

'Ever since I set foot in this high society of yours, I am enabled to understand present-day literature. Tell me how else, by what sort of poetry, could it arouse the curiosity of that Princess Mimi? With what sort of expertly honed catastrophe would you move her heart? What feeling could be intelligible to her, apart from repugnance? Yes, repugnance! That might be the only way through to her heart. Oh, that woman really instilled horror into me! Looking at her, I dressed her up in various outfits. What I mean is that I worked out a logical development of her ideas and feelings, pictured to myself how a spirit like hers would react in life's varying circumstances, and I got straight to… to the bonfires of the Inquisition!

'Don't laugh at me! Lavater[9] used to say: give me one line of a face, and I'll relate the whole person to you. Get for me just the extent to which someone delights in scandal, loves to seek out and tell all about household secrets, and all under the pretence of virtue, and I, with mathematical exactitude, will determine the extent of that person's immorality, emptiness of soul, absence of any real thought and any religious or noble feeling. My words are not overstatements; I agree, though, here with the church fathers. They know the human heart thoroughly. Just listen to the bitter regret with which they remember people like that, "Woe will befall them on Judgement Day", they say, "better for them not to know the sacred objects than to install a throne to the Devil amidst them".'

'Steady on, old boy! What's come over you? That all seems like a real homily!'

'Oh, do excuse me! All that which I saw and heard was so repulsive that I just had to let it all come out. By the way, tell me, though, did you really not catch Princess Mimi's conversation with that paid dancer?'

'No, I wasn't taking any notice.'

'You – and a literary man, too…? Yes, well, that oh, so nice a society conversation contained the germ of a thousand crimes, a thousand disasters!'

'Ah, well old boy! That was just when I was being told a rather more interesting story – about how one of my fellows in the service made his career…'

The carriage came to a stop.

3
THE RESULTS OF FAMILY CONVERSATIONS

> I speak, you speak, he speaks, we
> speak, you all speak, they all speak.
>
> The Works of… !?

Fortunately, not very many people shared the severe opinion of our anonymous orator on present-day society and therefore all its diminutive bits of business went on in their own sweet way without any kind of hindrance. And meanwhile, imperceptibly to anyone, that form of superstition which is known as time was moving on.

Countess Rifeyskaya, a long-term friend of the Baroness', had been attempting to make even closer friends with her from the time of Granitsky's arrival: they were to be seen together on outings and at the theatre. The Baroness knew nothing of the old acquaintance of Granitsky with the Countess; it's true that she did notice that they were not indifferent one to the other, but she regarded this as the usual brief flirtation which people, at times when they have nothing better to do, are liable to go in for. Should it be revealed? Well, the Baroness, imperceptibly to herself, was even rather pleased with her discovery: this struck her as a reliable tool of defence against assaults from the woman who was her enemy.

But Granitsky and the Countess carried on their business with a particular art, gained through experience of long duration: in society they were quite able to appear completely indifferent, one to the other. Talking to other people on completely extraneous subjects, they were quite able to nominate one to the other a meeting point, or convey some means or other of precaution; they were even quite able to make fun of each other at opportune moments. Their more fiery looks would be exchanged only through a mirror; but not a single minute did they waste: they would catch that very moment when other people's eyes were diverted to some other purpose. Precisely at an instantaneous exit from a room, or from the theatre, in short at any suitable occasion at all, their hands would come together, and often a loving kiss would reward their lengthy restraint, and this would be all the more intense for their ridiculing of social opinion.

Meanwhile, the seeds tossed around by the expert hand of Princess Mimi reproduced and multiplied, like those wonderful trees in a Brazilian virgin forest, which stretch out their boughs, and each bough falls to the ground and becomes a new tree, and once more it will bite into the ground with its branches, and there will be more, and yet more... And woe unto the imprudent wayfarer who gets caught in these innumerable interlacings! One young gasbag recounted the Princess Mimi conversation to another; this one passed it on to his mother, the mother to her best friend, and so it went on. Mimi had constructed just this sort of gallery around herself; the old Princess had a similar one; the Princess Mimi's old neighbour at the ball had the same thing. And these galleries grew and grew; eventually they would meet, interweave and enhance each other, and a closely woven network enclosed around the Baroness along with Granitsky, just like that with Mars and Venus. In this instance, all the tongues of the town which were at all capable of wagging began to wag: some from a wish to persuade their listeners that they were not implicated in those sort of sins; others from a dislike of the Baroness; others again, so as to make a laughing stock of her husband; and yet others just from a wish to demonstrate that they too were privy to drawing-room secrets.

Granitsky, occupied with his own strategic moves with the Countess, and the Baroness, reassured by what she had discovered, had no awareness of the storm that was preparing to break over them. They were not aware that every word of theirs, every movement of theirs, was being noted, discussed, talked up; they were not aware that there was to be found, right in front of their eyes, a law court made up from the bonnets of every fashion possible. Whenever the Baroness, without any formality, turned in a friendly way to Granitsky, the law court would decide that she was putting on the role of innocence. Whenever, by some dint of circumstance, throughout a whole evening she had no conversation at all with Granitsky, then the law court would find that this had been done so as to distract everyone's attention. Whenever Granitsky talked to the Baron, that would mean him wanting to neutralise the unfortunate husband's suspicion. Whenever he kept quiet, that meant that the lover was not capable of controlling his jealousy. In short, whatever the Baroness and Granitsky might do – whether he sat down beside her at the table or not, danced with her or did not dance with her, met up with her or did not meet up with her on outings, whether the Baroness was particularly amiable or not to her husband in front of other people, whether she drove out with him or did not – everything for this spare-time law court was evidence to corroborate its conclusions.

And as for the poor Baron! If he had known what tender concern the ladies showed for him, if he had known of all the virtues uncovered by them in his personage! His customary drowsiness was considered the internal anguish of a passionate husband; his gormless smile a sign of unaffected benevolence; in his drowsy eyes they found sagacity; in his passion for whist – a desire not to notice his wife's unfaithfulness, or to keep up appearances.

One day, in the home of a mutual friend, Baroness Dauerthal encountered Princess Mimi. Of course, they were only too pleased, shook each other's hands in a very friendly way, put to each other an infinite number of questions and on both sides left these almost entirely without answer. In short, there was no hint of hostility, no hint of recollecting any episode at the ball – it was as though for a whole age they had never stopped being staunch friends. In the drawing room, apart from them, there were not many guests – only an old Princess, Mimi's young widowed sister, her old and regular ballroom neighbour, plus Granitsky, and just two or three more.

For the whole day, Granitsky had been dragging himself around various drawing rooms, so as to come across his Countess and, not having caught up with her anywhere, was feeling bored and off-handed. It had been very disagreeable for the Baroness to meet up with Princess Mimi, as it had been for the old Princess with the Baroness. Mimi alone was very glad of an opportune moment for observing the Baroness and Granitsky within a small circle. Due to all this, there arose in the drawing room an intolerable disquiet: the conversation passed continually from one topic to another, and was continually interrupted. The hostess was dredging up all the old news, since everything that could be, regarding the new, had already been said, and everyone was just looking at her while evidently not listening.

Mimi was in her element: while talking to others, she didn't miss as much as a word from the Baroness or Granitsky, and in each word she would find a key to the hieroglyphic discourse usually being used in such concerns. Granitsky's perceptible off-handedness she interpreted as either a minor quarrel between the lovers, or to suspicion having been aroused in the husband. And the Baroness! Not the slightest gesture of hers eluded Mimi's attentive observation, and each one of these told her the whole story in all its details. Meanwhile, the poor Baroness, as if she were a guilty party, turned away from Granitsky: first she would hardly make any reply to what he said, then she would suddenly turn to him with questions. She could not resist glancing now and then at Princess Mimi, and frequently, when their eyes met sideways, the Baroness fell into a state of unwitting confusion, which only increased from her anger at herself for feeling confused.

A little while later, Granitsky looked at the clock, said that he was off to the opera, and vanished.

'Well, we really upset that little appointment of theirs,' Mimi said quietly to her ever-present neighbour. 'But still, they will keep on!'

Granitsky had hardly gone out, when a servant informed the Baroness that her carriage, for which she had been waiting for some time, had now arrived.

At that minute a vague sort of idea ran through Princess Mimi's mind: she herself could scarcely take account of it. It was a dark, random inspiration of malevolence – it was the feeling of someone who will stake a hundred to one in the certain hope of not winning.

'I have a dreadful headache!' she said. 'Please, Baroness, let your carriage take me home, just a street away: we have let ours go.'

Their mutual looks understood each other. The Baroness instinctively guessed what was going on within Princess Mimi. At the same time, she did not fathom anything clearly as to the latter's intention; yet – herself not knowing from what – felt afraid. Naturally, she created no difficulty in agreeing to Mimi's suggestion, but her face flushed, and flushed so much that everyone noticed. All of this occurred a hundred times faster than we have just been able to recount the scene.

Outside there was a strong snowstorm. The wind was blowing out the streetlights, and at two steps you couldn't make out a human being. Muffled from head to toe in her big coat, Mimi, her heart a-tremble, mounted the carriage steps, supported by two lackeys. She had hardly taken two steps up, when suddenly from inside the carriage a big male hand grabbed her by the hand, to help her in. Mimi threw herself backwards, cried out – and this was all but a cry of joy! She ran like a shot back up the staircase and, in quite a state, gasping from various feelings blazing up within her, she rushed over to her sister Maria, who, from her scream, heard throughout the house, had been impelled, together with the other ladies, to run out of the drawing room.

'You can talk!' she whispered to her sister, but so that everyone could hear, 'Keep standing up for your Baroness! She's got... in that carriage... that Granitsky of hers. You could advise her at least to conduct her appointments with a bit more care, and not to expose me to such shame...'

The Baroness was drawn over to the noise. Mimi hushed up and, as though unconscious, threw herself into an armchair. While the Baroness was asking the Princess, to no avail, what had befallen her – the door opened and –

But, allow me, kindest sirs and *mesdames*! I consider that now is the most opportune moment to get you to read this –

PREFACE

C'est avoir l'esprit de son âge![10]

Some little while ago, there came into use, and it has already had time to fall into disuse, the practice of writing a preface in the middle of a book. I consider this to be a splendid practice, that is to say very advantageous to the author. It used to be the case that a writer would kneel down, ask and implore the reader to pay some attention to him; but the reader would smugly flick over a few pages and mercilessly leave the writer in his undignified posture. In our age of justice and reckoning, the writer in a preface makes the reader kneel, or picks on that moment when readers themselves will kneel down, pleading to know the outcome. Then the writer pompously puts on his doctoral hood and demonstrates to the reader just why he should be kneeling – all this with the innocent intention of obliging the reader to read through the preface. Like it or not, this is a splendid method, for anyone who has not read the preface will know just half the book. So then, dearest readers, get down on your knees, get reading, read with the deepest attention and the deepest respect, because I am going to be telling you what you all have long since already known.

Do you know, dearest gentle-readers, that writing books is a very difficult business?

That out of all books the most difficult for a writer are novels and tales?

That of novels and novellas, the most difficult are those which have to be written in Russian?

That of novels written in Russian, the most difficult are those in which the conduct of present-day society is being described?

Leaving out a thousand reasons for such difficulties, I will say something about the one thousand and first.

This ... reason – excuse me! – *pardon*! – *verzeihen Sie*! – *scusate*! – *forgive me*! – This reason is: that our ladies do not speak in Russian!!

Just listen, my dearest ladies: I am not a student, not a schoolboy, not a publisher, neither A, nor B. I do not belong to any literary school and do not even believe in the existence of Russian belles-lettres. I myself speak in Russian only rarely; I express myself in French almost without mistakes; I blurt it out in the purest Parisian speech. In short, I am a decent enough fellow – and I can assure you that it is shameful, humiliating and improper not to speak in Russian! I know that French is already beginning to go out of fashion: but what unclean spirit whispered that it should be replaced not by Russian, but by that blasted English, on which one has to break one's tongue, clench one's teeth, and exhibit frontward one's lower jaw? And, due to that prerequisite, isn't it farewell to that pretty little mouth with the fresh, pink little Slavic lips? It would be better to be without one.

You know just as well as I do that strong passions operate in society – passions from which people turn pale, or red, or yellow, become exhausted and even die. But, at the highest levels of the social stratosphere, these passions are expressed by just a phrase, just a word, just a conventional word which, as with the alphabet, is neither to be converted nor fabricated. A novelist of sufficient conscience not to be able to bring himself to project an Eskimo conversation as the language of society must know this social code to perfection, must devour all these conventional words, because, I repeat, it is not possible to fabricate them. They get born in the incandescence of high-society conversation, and the meaning attached to them at that minute will remain with them for all time. But where in a Russian drawing room will you catch such a word? This is where all the Russian passions, thoughts, derision, annoyance, the slightest gesture of the soul, get expressed in well-prepared words taken from the rich French store, which the French novelists exploit so artfully, and to which they (talent aside) owe the greater part of their success. How often they can make do without all those lengthy descriptions, explanations and preparatory passages which are a torment both for the writer and the reader, and which they easily supplant with a few high-life phrases understandable to all! Those who have some idea of the technicalities of the composition of a novel, they will grasp all the advantages produced by this situation.

Just ask our poet,* one of the few Russian writers who really know the Russian language, why, in his verses, he has used as an entity the word *vulgar*, or *vulgaire*. This word depicts in half a person's character, and in half that person's lot. But, to get this over in Russian, one would have to scrawl a couple of pages of explanation – and what a snappy task that would be for the writer, and what fun for the reader! That's just one example for you, but it would be possible to find a thousand. And that's why I ask my readers to have some regard for all these circumstances and not to blame me if, for some, my characters' conversations are too bookish, and for others not sufficiently grammatical. As far as the latter goes, I will cite Griboedov, just about the only writer, in my view, who really grasped the secret of rendering our conversational language on paper.

After that I apologise to my readers if I have bored them by confiding to their generous disposition these trite and, in the fullest sense of the word, domestic impediments, and by showing off the emplacements upon which novelistic scenes start moving. I come on, in this situation, like the director of some poor provincial theatre. Brought to desperation by the impatience of his audience, who were bored stiff in a lengthy interval, he took it upon himself to raise the curtain and show them indeed how hard it is to turn clouds into the sea, a blanket into a regal awning, a housekeeper into a princess and any old rogue into a *premier ingénu*.[11] The gracious audience found this a more fascinating spectacle than the play itself. And that's the way I see it, too.

Of course, some people get born with unusual talents, for whom everything is ready formed – the social manners, the course of the novel, the language and the characters. If there's a need to depict a person from high society or, as they might say, of fashionable tone – nothing could be easier! They will certainly send him somewhere abroad; for greater authenticity of habit they will make him not be in government employment, sleep until two in the afternoon, wander round the cake shops, and drink until dinner – champagne, naturally. If conversation in decent society is called for – easier still! Throw open Mme Genlis' first translated novel,[12] add into the necessary places the words *mon cher*, *ma chère*, *bonjour*, *comment vous portez-vous*[13] – and the conversation is done! But nature bestows such exactitude in description and such a true and perspicacious gaze on just a few geniuses. I was ill-starred by her in that respect, and accordingly I simply ask my reader not to hold it against me if, in some of my genteel domestic conversations, I have not succeeded in fully preserving an authentic high-society colour. And to the ladies, I repeat my categorical request to speak in Russian.

By not speaking in Russian they deprive themselves of a great many benefits:

I. They are unable to comprehend our literary compositions as well as they might; but as for the most part they can be congratulated on this, we will let that matter pass.

II. If they, notwithstanding my exhortations, will still not speak in Russian, then I – I – from now on, I will not write a single novella for them: they can just read Messrs A, B, C and the rest.

Confident that this threat will have a stronger effect on my lady readers than any proofs positive, I shall return composedly to my story.

And so, the door opened, and ... in tumbled the old Baron, understanding not a thing to do with this venture. He had come over for his wife and, as he was intending to go on somewhere or other with her straight away, due to some unforeseen circumstance, he had chosen to stay in the carriage and not announce himself to the hostess. The scream from Princess Mimi, whom he had at first taken for his wife, had forced him to emerge.

But such was the magnetic influence whipped up by both the city-wide rumours and all the foregoing, that everyone just looked at him without believing their eyes. It was some little time later, after a glass of water, after eau de cologne, Hoffmann drops and suchlike remedies, before they all deemed that, on such occasions, one just had to laugh. I am sure that many of my readers will have noticed, on varying occasions in life, the influence this magnetism can have, provoking a strong conviction amid a crowd of people for almost no visible reason. Having been exposed to this influence, we then in vain do our utmost to destroy it through common sense. Blind persuasion

* Need I remind the reader that the allusion here is to Pushkin's Onegin? [Author's note.]

so takes possession of our will that, within us, common sense itself unwittingly starts to ferret out any circumstances that may corroborate this conviction. At such times, the most absurd spoken word can have a great impact. Sometimes this very word might be forgotten, yet the impression it has produced will remain in the mind and, unnoticeably to the person concerned, give birth to a series of thoughts that would never have entered the head but for that word, and to which it may bear only a distant connection. This magnetism plays a very important role in prominent, as in the most trifling of happenings and, perhaps, for many such must serve as the sole explanation. This is what happened this time. The occurrence with the Princess was quite simple and straightforward, but the predilection of all those in attendance for another kind of solution was so strong that, in the case of many of them, at one and the same time, there arose a vague notion: as though the Baron had turned up here as a sort of *godfather*. By what means this could have occurred, at that moment no one was in any state to explain; but subsequently this idea developed and gathered strength, while common sense, together with memory, hunted out from the past a plenitude of corroborations for what was in reality just an isolated blind persuasion.

If only you knew what an uproar was raised in the city after this event! In every nook and cranny, with a whisper or a shout, over the embroidery design, over a book, in the theatre, or in front of the holy altar, male and female conversationalists talked, paraphrased, explicated, quarrelled, and went haywire. A fire in the heavens would not have made on them a much stronger impression! And all of this – just from a husband taking it into his head to come and collect his wife. Observing such deplorable phenomena, you end up in total amazement. What does attract these people to matters that are of no concern to them? What is it that makes these people, these soulless people, ice-cold at the sight of the noblest or the meanest of actions, or the highest or the most vulgar of ideas, before the most elegant of artworks, or the violation of all the laws of nature and of humanity – how is it that these people can become inflamed, profound, perspicacious and eloquent when it's a matter of a decoration, rank, a wedding, some family secret or other, or something which they have simply wrung out from their withered brains in the name of decency?

4
RESCUING ADVICE

Master: You fool! That should have been done on the side.
Servant: That's just what I did, sir, I came at him from the side.

The old Baron had a junior brother, many years younger than himself, an officer and generally a really nice young chap.

To describe his character is rather difficult: it is necessary to start from some way back.

Well, you see, honest people taught our fathers that one has to doubt everything, reckoning one's every action, steer clear of all systems and of all futilites, and search everywhere for the essential benefit – or, as they would say then: cull from near at hand and don't stray too far. Our fathers did as they were told, left aside all futile things, which I won't spell out, so as not to be taken for a pedant, and they were only too pleased that the entire wisdom of humankind could be limited to dinner and supper, and other such similarly utilitarian matters. Meanwhile, our fathers produced children; the question of their upbringing arose. They themselves sagaciously carried on doubting everything, laughing at systems and occupying themselves only with utilitarian matters. Meanwhile their children grew and grew, and, contrary to the honest people, formulated their own system of life. However, this was no mere dreamlike system, but one which found a place for an epigram of Voltaire, an anecdote related by grandmother, a line of Parny's verse, a moralistic-arithmetical phrase from Bentham, a derisive memoir of an example of literary platitude, an article from a newspaper, a bloody statement by Napoleon, a law concerning card-playing honour, and other things like that, with which, up until now, old and young neophytes of the eighteenth century still make do.

The younger Baron had this system at his fingertips. He could not fall in love: to him there was something ludicrous in this sensation. He simply loved women, all of them with just a few exceptions; his setter dog; Lepage guns; and his good friends, when they didn't get on his nerves. He believed that two times two makes four, that a vacancy for him as a Captain would soon come up, and that tomorrow he was due to dance in numbers two, five and six of the contradance.

However, let's be fair; the young man had a noble, fervid and kindly soul. But what has the criminal upbringing of this decayed and perfume-drenched age not shattered? Rejoice, people of reckoning, doubt and the essential benefit! Rejoice, defenders of a derisive disbelief in anything sacred! Your fancies have surged forth, have flooded everything, enlightenment and ignorance alike. Where can we expect to see the sun, which has to dry up this bog and turn it into fecund earth?

In a room covered with hanging Parisian lithographs and Asiatic daggers, in a curving armchair and clothed in a tight-fitting kaftan, now looking at the clock, now flicking over the pages of a French vaudeville, lay the young Baron.

His man handed him a note.

'From whom?'

'From the Marquise de Créquis.'

'From my auntie?'

The note had the following content.

'Drop round to me today after dinner, my dear boy. But don't forget, as you are accustomed to doing; I have something to discuss with you, and it's very important.'

'Oh well,' muttered to himself the young man, 'Auntie has contrived yet some other cousin who will need to be led out on to the parquet! Oh, all these cousins of mine! Where on earth do they all come from…? Tell my aunt,' he said loudly, 'that that's fine – I'll be there. Now to get dressed.'

When the young Baron Dauerthal appeared before the Marquise, she put aside her large knitting needles, took him by the hand and, with a mysterious look, led him through a whole row of rooms excelling in a characteristic lack of taste, over to her cabinet. Here she seated him on a small divan encircled by pots of geraniums, balsam, mint and family portraits. The air was permeated with eau de cologne and spermaceti.

'Tell me, Auntie,' the young man asked her, 'what is all this in aid of? You're not wanting to marry me off, are you?'

'Not just yet, my darling! But, joking aside, I do have to talk to you very, very seriously. Tell me, please be so good, what about this friend of yours – Granitsky, isn't it? What's he like…?'

'Yes, Granitsky. He's an excellent young man, a good family…'

'Not one I've ever heard of. Tell me, how do you come to be such close friends?'

'In a little place in Italy, when I was worn out, hungry and a bit ill, I couldn't get a room at the inn: and he shared his with me. I then became quite ill: he looked after me for a whole week and lent me money. I got him to give his word to stay with me whenever he would come to Petersburg: that's how we got to know each other… But what are all these questions for, Auntie?'

'Just listen, my dear boy! All that is just fine; I can quite understand that some Granitsky would be only too glad to do a good turn for a Baron Dauerthal.'

'Auntie, you are talking about my real friend!' the young man broke in with some dissatisfaction.

'That's all just fine, my dear boy! I am not condemning your real friend. The way he treated you was very honourable on his part. But permit me to tell you something quite candidly: you are a young man, barely entering the social world. You must take care in your choice of acquaintances. Young people these days are so dissolute.'

'I would think, Auntie, no more and no less than they ever were…'

'Not at all! Before, at least there was more deference towards one's relations; family ties were not like now – they were closer…'

'And even sometimes too close, my dearest Auntie, isn't that right?'

'That's not right! But that's not the point. Permit me to remark to you that, in this instance, the one we are talking about, you acted very impulsively: you came across and got mixed up with a person whom no one knows. Is he at least in one of the services somewhere?'

'No.'

'Well, you tell me, in that case, what sort of a person that makes him! He is not even serving! That's probably because they won't take him on anywhere.'

'You've got it wrong, Auntie. He isn't in any of the services because his mother is Italian and all his estates are in Italy. He can't just leave her, and that's actually due to family ties…'

'Then why is he here?'

'On business for his father. But tell me, for goodness' sake, where are all these questions leading?'

'In a nutshell, dear boy, your friendship with this person gives me great displeasure, and you would be doing me a great favour, if … well, if you would just throw him out of the house.'

'For pity's sake, Auntie! You know that I do everything, absolutely as you tell me to, but put yourself in my position. Why ever should I suddenly turn against a person to whom I owe so much and, for no obvious reason chase him out of the house? Say what you like, but I just can't take such an ungrateful step.'

'That's all just rubbish, dear boy! Novelistic ideas, and nothing more! There is a way, and an extremely polite one, of showing him that he is just an encumbrance upon you.'

'No doubt, Auntie, that would be very easy to do; but I tell you again that I could not take such foul ingratitude upon my conscience. Say what you will, but I can't, there's no way that I could...'

'Just listen!' replied the Marquise after a brief silence. 'You are aware of everything that you are obliged to your brother for...'

'Auntie!'

'Don't interrupt me. You know that, after the death of your father, he could have grabbed hold of your whole estate. He didn't do that, he took you into his arms, aged three, brought you up, and tied up all the loose business ends. When you had grown up, he got you into the service, and honourably shared the estate out with you. In short, you owe everything, your very entirety, to him...'

'Auntie, what are you actually saying?'

'Listen, you are no longer a child and you are by no means a stupid chap, but you are compelling me to tell you what I would rather not say.'

'And what is that, Auntie?'

'Just listen! First promise me not to do anything foolhardy, but to act just as a sensible person should act.'

'For God's sake, just say what you have to say, Auntie!'

'I have confidence in you, and that is why I am asking you, whether you might not have noticed something between the Baroness and your Granitsky?'

'With the Baroness! What is that supposed to mean?'

'Your Granitsky is having a love affair with her...'

'Granitsky? ... That's not possible!'

'I am not trying to deceive you. That is the case: your brother has been dishonoured, his grey hairs have been desecrated.'

'But there would have to be proof...'

'What do you mean, proof? I'm already getting letters about this from Liflandia. Everyone is sorry for your brother and surprised that you can assist in his betrayal.'

'Me? Betraying him? That's libel, Auntie, pure libel. Who had the audacity to write that to you?'

'That, I'm not going to tell you. But I'm leaving it to you just to decide whether Granitsky can remain in your house. Your debt obliges you, before this relationship becomes even more public, to try by courteous means to get him to move out of your house and, if at all possible, out of Russia. You realise that this has to happen without any fuss; just find some pretext or other...'

'Rest assured that this will all be done, Auntie. I am grateful to you for the information. My brother is now old and frail; this is my business, my duty... Goodbye...'

'Wait a minute, just a minute! Don't get impulsive! What's needed here is not impulsiveness, but composure. You will promise me not do anything foolhardy, to act just as a sensible person should act, and not as a child?'

'Oh, don't worry, Auntie! I'll settle everything in the best way possible. Goodbye.'

'Don't forget that you have to act very cautiously in this matter!' the Marquise shouted after him. 'Have a quiet word with Granitsky, don't get impulsive. Bring the matter up on the side, beat about the bush a bit... Do you understand?'

'Don't worry, don't worry, Auntie!' replied the Baron, rushing out.

The blood was rushing around the young man's head.

5
THE FUTURE

> *...l'avenir n'est à personne, Sire,*
> *l'avenir est à Dieu.*[14]
>
> Victor Hugo

Throughout this scene, there was another one going on.

In the interior of a huge house, situated behind a splendid shop, was to be found quite a small room with a single window hung with a blind, looking on to the courtyard. From the appearance of the room, it would be hard to guess to whom it belonged: plain plaster walls, a low ceiling, a few old chairs and an enormous mirror. In the alcove was a sumptuous divan with all the elaborations of luxury, a low armchair with a curved back – all of these features seemed somehow to be in dispute amongst themselves. One door of the room, through a concealed corridor, connected with the shop; the other went out on to the street opposite.

A young man paced around the room with quick steps and he often stopped, either in the middle or by the doors, carefully listening. This was Granitsky.

Suddenly a rustle was heard, the door opened, and an attractive woman, attractively dressed, threw herself into his embraces. This was the Countess Lydia Rifeyskaya.

'You know, don't you, Gabriel,' she said hurriedly to him, 'that you and I are seeing each other here for the last time?'

'The last time?' the young man exclaimed. 'But wait a minute! What's wrong with you? You are so pale!'

'It's nothing. I got a bit cold. In my hurry to see you, I forgot to put my boots on. That corridor is so cold... It's nothing!'

'How careless you are! Your health mustn't be neglected...'

The young man moved the armchair towards the fireplace, seated the attractive woman upon it, took her shoes off, and was trying to warm up her delightful little feet with his breath.

'Oh, do stop it, Gabriel! These minutes are precious. I was only able to tear myself away from the house with great difficulty. I have come to see you with some important news. My husband has had a second stroke and, I hate to say it, the doctors have told me that my husband will not recover from it. His tongue is paralysed, his face has gone twisted; he looks terrible! The poor thing, he can't even say a word!… He can hardly lift his hand! You can't believe how pitiful I find him.'

And the Countess covered her face with her hands. At the same time, Gabriel was kissing her frozen – as though made from white marble – little feet, and clasping them to his burning cheeks.

'Lydia,' he said, 'Lydia! You will be free…'

'Oh, say that to me more often, Gabriel! That is the only notion that can, for a moment, make me forget my situation. But there is something awful in that thought. So as to be happy in your embraces, it is necessary for me to step across a coffin…! For my happiness, I need a man's death…! I have to want this death…! It's just dreadful, dreadful! It turns my heart upside down, it's against nature.'

'But Lydia, if there is anyone guilty here, it really is not you. You are as innocent as an angel; they gave you away in marriage against your will. Remember the extent to which you stood up against your parents, remember all your agonies, all our agony…'

'Oh, Gabriel, I do know all that; and when I think about the past my conscience is clear. God knows what I have had to endure in my life! But when I cast a glance at my husband, at his contorted face, at his shaking hand; when he tries to beckon me over, me, in whom for six whole years he has aroused only one feeling – one of revulsion; when I recall having always deceived him, and that I am deceiving him now, then I forget what chain of agonies, moral and physical, drove me to this deception. I just wilt between these two perceptions – and the one cannot dominate over the other!'

Granitsky remained quiet. There would have been no point in him trying to console Lydia at this moment.

'Don't be angry with me, Gabriel!' she said finally, nestling his head. 'You understand me; from our childhood you have been used to understanding me. You are the only person I can confide my agonies to...'

And she ardently clasped him against her bosom.

'But that's enough! Time is flying. I can't stay here any longer... Here is my last kiss for you! Now listen: I am sure we shall be happy; I am sure that, what the despotism of society took from us, Providence will return. But, until that day comes, I belong entirely to my husband. From now on, through unrelenting care, through long sleepless nights by his bedside, and through the agony of not seeing you, I have to redeem our love and entreat our happiness from God. Don't try to see me, don't write to me; let me forget you. I shall then become calmer, and my conscience will torment me less. I will then more easily be able to think of myself as completely clean and innocent... Goodbye! Just a couple more words: don't change anything in the way you live, carry on doing the rounds, dance, flirt a bit, just as if no change were in the offing... Call in today on my husband, but I shan't receive you, as you're not related. So, just do the rounds today and tell everyone apathetically about his illness. Goodbye!'

'Wait a moment! Lydia! One more kiss...! How many long days will it be...'

'Oh, don't make me think any more about that...! Goodbye. Be more patient than I will be. Just remember, the time will come, when I won't have to say to you, "people are coming – go away, Gabriel!" Oh, but it's horrible! Just horrible!'

And so they parted.

6
THIS COULD HAVE BEEN FORESEEN

'Vous allez me rabacher je ne sais quels lieux communs de morale, que tous ont dans la bouche, qu'on fait sonner bien, haut, pourvu que personne ne soit obligé de les pratiquer.'

'Mais s'ils se jettent dans le crime?'

'C'est de leur condition.'[15]

Le neveu de Rameau

It was in a state of considerable agitation that the young Baron Dauerthal returned home.

'Is Granitsky at home?' he asked.

'No, he's not, sir.'

'Tell me, just as soon as he arrives.'

At this point, he recalled that Granitsky was due to be going to B***'s that evening.

All the minutes spent waiting were dreadful for the young man. He felt as though, for the first time in his life, he had been called for important business; that this couldn't be got out of by tossing off an epigram, or through apathy, or just a smile. Here he needed powerful feelings, to think powerfully, to concentrate all the powers in his soul; in short, he needed to take action, to take action himself, without requiring advice or expecting support. But this sort of stress was unknown to him; he could not really answer to himself for his own thoughts. His blood was just blazing up, and his heart was just beating faster. He imagined, as though in a dream, the ongoing talk of the town: his brother with his grey hair, humiliated and weak; his own wish to demonstrate his love and gratitude to the older man; his comrades, his epaulettes, sword and boyish anger;

the wish to demonstrate that he was no longer a child; the idea that murder can expiate every crime. All these reveries interchanged, one after the other, but everything remained dim and indeterminate: he did not know how to seek an answer from that law court which, not dependent on temporal prejudices and opinions, always pronounces exactly and truly. His upbringing had forgotten to apprise him of that court, and life had not taught him to inquire about it. The language of this court was an unknown quantity to the Baron.

Finally, the hour struck. The young man rushed to his carriage, galloped away, found Granitsky, took him by the arm, led him out of the crowd to a distant room and … then did not know what to say to him. Eventually he remembered his aunt's words and, attempting to put on a cold-blooded expression, muttered:

'You're going to Italy!'

'Not yet,' replied Granitsky, having taken this for a question and looking at him with some surprise.

'You have to go to Italy! Do you understand what I am saying?'

'Not in the least!'

'I want you to go to Italy!' said the Baron in a raised voice. 'Now do you understand?'

'Tell me, if you will be so kind: what is it, have you gone mad, or something?'

'There are some people, whom I shall not name, for whom any noble quality amounts to madness…'

'Baron, you don't know what you are saying. Your words have the whiff of gunpowder.'

'It's a whiff I'm quite used to.'

'On manoeuvres?'

'That we shall see.'

The Baron's eyes started to flash. Things were already getting to the stage of personal insult.

They got everyone who had come into the room towards the end of the conversation to give their word to keep it a secret, returned again to the hall, did a few turns at a waltz, and disappeared.

Within a few hours, their seconds were already measuring out the paces and loading the pistols.

Granitsky went up to the Baron.

'Before we send one another to the next world, I would be fascinated to find out what we are shooting at each other for.'

The Baron led his opponent to one side, away from the seconds.

'That must be more comprehensible to you than it is to me…' he said.

'Not in the least.'

'If I were to name a certain woman to you…'

'A woman…! But which woman?'

'That's really too much! The wife of my brother, my old and ill brother, my benefactor… Do you understand?'

'Now, after that, I understand absolutely not a thing!'

'That's strange! The whole town is saying that you have dishonoured my brother; he has become a laughing stock…'

'Baron, they have shamelessly deceived you! I am asking you to name to me this deceiver.'

'It was a woman who told me.'

'Baron, you have acted very precipitately. If you had asked me at the outset, I would have told you of my situation. But now it's too late, we have to duel. But I don't want to die leaving you deceived. Here is my hand, that I have never even given the Baroness a thought.'

The young Baron was in a state of great embarrassment throughout the conversation: he liked Granitsky, knew all about his nobility, believed that he was not deceiving him, and just cursed – himself, Auntie, and the whole social world.

One of the seconds, a veteran duellist, very severe in things of this sort, said, 'Well, then, gentlemen! Things with you seem to be looking up a bit, don't they? And so much the better: make it up, make it up; that's the best thing, really…'

These words were said very straightforwardly, but to the Baron they seemed like a taunt – or perhaps there really was something taunting in the second's tone of voice. Blood rushed to the young man's brain.

'Oh, no!' he exclaimed, scarcely knowing himself what he was saying. 'No, we are not thinking of making up. We have an important clarification to resolve…'

The last words again reminded the young man of his criminal irresponsibility: beside himself, shaken up by unaccountable emotions, for the second time he led his opponent to one side.

'Granitsky!' he said to him, 'I have acted like a child. What is there left for us to do?'

'I don't know,' Granitsky replied.

'Tell the seconds of our peculiar mistake…?'

'That would be spreading the rumours about your brother's wife.'

'You mocked my bravery; the seconds know that.'

'You were speaking to me in such a tone…'

'It cannot be left like this.'

'It can't be left like this.'

'They would just say that we spilled not blood, but champagne in our duel…'

'Let's try to give each other just a scratch.'

They stepped up to the barrier. One, two, three! Granitsky's bullet scratched the Baron's arm; Granitsky fell dead.

7
CONCLUSION

> There exist enthusiasts for the defence of everyone and everything: they don't want to see the bad in anything. These people are extremely harmful...
>
> A High Society Judgement

Every reader is probably already guessing what was the upshot of this whole story.

For as long as men only knew of the duel, then it was attributed just to Granitsky's mocking of the young Baron's bravery; the rumours over this differed. However, when the moral ladies, as described by us above, got to know of this event, all misconceptions came to an end. The true cause was tracked down at once, investigated, processed, embellished with annotating comments and disseminated through all possible means.

The poor Baroness could not withstand this cruel persecution. Her honour, the sole emotion within her which was alive and sacred; her honour, for which she had surrendered all the ideas entering her mind, and all the impulses of a youthful heart: her honour had been outraged – through no fault of hers, and irreversibly. The Baroness took to her bed.

The young Baron and the pair of seconds were dispatched into exile – far from all the enjoyments of the society life which for them could be the sole source of happiness.

The Countess Rifeyskaya remained a widow.

There is behaviour that gets persecuted by society: the guilty perish, the innocent perish. There are people who sow the seeds of calamity from full hands, who incite an aversion for humanity in the souls of people high and tender, who, in short, exultantly file away at society's foundations, and society keeps them close to its bosom, like a fatuous sun which apathetically comes up equally above the shouts of battle as above the wise man's prayer.

A card coterie had been assembled for Princess Mimi – she had already refused any dancing. A young man came up to the green table.

'This morning the sufferings of Baroness Dauerthal finally came to an end!' he said. 'The ladies here will be able to pride themselves on their having so skilfully done her to death.'

'What impertinence!' one of them whispered to another.

'It was no such thing!' retorted Princess Mimi, covering her card trick, 'killing is done not by people, but by lawless passions.'

'Oh, that's beyond doubt!' remarked many.

Princess Zizi

(Dedicated to E.A. Sukhozanet[16]*)*
Sometimes in the domestic circle heroism is needed more than it is in the most brilliant profession in life. The domestic circle, for a woman, is the field of honour and sacred exploits. Why do so few understand this…?

A woman's words

'Where have you sprung from?'

'From the exchange.'

'And, so?'

'It's higher every day!'

'So much the better.'

'How is it better? From that I am losing 20,500 roubles.'

'Losing?'

'Oh, what's the use of talking to you! You won't understand me...'

'But, still...'

'Well, you see: I now have 120,500 roubles of free money. For 100,000 I am buying land for my village in Tula province. For 20,500 I wanted to buy shares in a new insurance company, but they've now gone up so much that it's not worth it, and I am left having to hold on to my 20,500, virtually without any use at all.'

'And that's what you call losing 20,000...?'

'Oh, I already told you, you wouldn't understand a thing!'

With these words my friend, who belongs to the new breed of fashionable industrialists, threw himself into his armchair, plunged himself into pensiveness, and twisted his moustache with annoyance.

'Do you have a touch of spleen today?' I asked him.

'Yes, spleen, and pretty bad, too... What are you laughing at?'

'I'm not laughing, but just observing how Byronism is combining with the exchange. If that dark industrial spirit had begun breathing over our generation as well, what would become of the new one?'

'The new one will be cleverer than ours. It will not waste so much time, and especially not so much money, on dreams, on loud-spoken words and on philanthropic ravings. It will rather occupy itself with solid, positive matters...'

'Tell me, though – you seem to have been writing elegies in your old age…?'

'Naturally! And they've been on about these in the papers, saying that they "expose in me a decisive tendency towards the elegiac ilk"…'

'Yes, indeed: you now seem to be looking like an elegiac poet… And you, of course, have been known to be in love…?'

'I don't give up on that, even now.'

'I know that, and this is demonstrated by your collection of letters over several volumes. Only, look out! Perhaps I should steal it one day, if only to examine how you can be attractive to the ladies and how all these polyglot rivals could get on, crammed between the same covers? But, no, joking aside, I have long been wanting to ask you: have you ever been really in love, a just once in a lifetime love, as this would be understood by those who concern themselves with the writing of novels, fairy tales and all that sort of thing?'

My industrialist stood up.

'I've no time to talk about that now,' he said. 'I'll have to say goodbye: I have to go and call on a certain man who has promised to get me the shares a bit cheaper.'

'Wait a minute! Who are you going to catch in now? It's five o'clock already. Have dinner here with me, and we'll try that new wine which I've been urged to buy. And, while we're at it, you can tell me…'

'Ah! So that's why you want to keep me back: stories are being demanded from you, *et le baron s'embarrasse.*[17] Your briefcase and your head are empty; you think you might stumble across some bright idea out of my jabberings.'

'Perhaps; and, if so, what's it to you? It's my equivalent of speculation on the stock exchange.'

'All right, I'll play it your way; I'll sentimentalise. Only order dinner pretty quickly. I repeat, I don't really have the time.'

After several glasses of wine, my friend did indeed rather soften up. Wine is a wonderful thing; it is the one and only poetic aspect of our century. If it be harmful in a physical respect, as the homeopaths affirm, then it's essential in the moral sense. It yanks off from a man, at least for a few minutes, his industrial, thrifty shell. It brings his natural state up to the surface and can often help you uncover, beneath a cold and sarcastic person, another one altogether – one who has both soul and heart, or even nothing resembling either the one or the other. Take our wine away from us, and we would be worse than the Chinese and the Americans.

'Yes, I have been in love,' my narrator finally said, 'that is to say in love in the way you mean, and so in love that even to this day I cannot get out of the unseemly habit of sighing, whenever I think of my beauty... My beauty! ... But hang on, I don't want to be telling you the end before the beginning. I myself, I quite admit, love starting a novel from its fourth part, but I know from experience that this brings neither profit nor pleasure. Besides, we need to have the historical evidence for you to see. Send your man over to my place, to bring back my green briefcase, the one lying beside the shaving table.

'In the year 18... I had returned to Moscow from foreign parts. I hadn't seen my homeland for ten years, and so everything was new for me: the streets, the buildings and the people. Guests gathered every evening in my guardian's drawing room. Their pastimes were the usual ones: drinking tea, playing whist and relating all the latest town gossip. Many of these tales aroused the most lively concern in everyone there, but for me, quite naturally, all this for ages was double

Dutch. I could grasp neither the conventional terms, nor the hints about families, nor the amusement caused by the names which reached my ears – in short, I got from it all nothing that allows social conversation to live. As you know, I am not one of those people who bring back from foreign parts a total indifference to everything at home, and for whom their own homeland is just as incomprehensible as the foreign lands had been. I had no wish to be a complete outsider in my family circle, so I was trying to pay heed to these perfectly everyday stories and I was almost picking up on all the names. One of these, I don't know how, particularly attracted my attention; this name was *Princess Zizi*. It reminded me of the inimitable Griboedov,[18] provoking thoughts about how pointless are your taunts, those of you esteemed authors, on the strange habit of name distortion. Or else in that name there was something special, but anyway I unwittingly moved my armchair up towards the circle when that name was pronounced.

'This is how the conversation about her went.'

'"Princess Zizi is getting married," said one of my cousins.

"To whom?"

"To some rural landowner or other."

"That would be a very good thing for her to do," remarked my aunt.

"That would be a pity! She's a very clever girl," someone remarked.

"She's a really odd one," remarked one lady.

"A true Christian."

"A true hypocrite, a real sham."

"A really nice..."

"An over-proud..."

"She's just waiting for some crown prince to marry her," muttered an elderly lady, having cast an involuntary glance at her son, himself an elderly enough "archival youth", now preparing himself for the diplomatic corps.

"For goodness' sake!" replied another such, with evidently spiteful intent, "whoever wants to marry her, anyway? Perhaps some madman or other? She has nothing at all..."

"Excuse me, but she's extremely well off."

"Nothing but bugbears, old chap, and an abyss of debts."

"I can assure you," to his partner, and adopting a significant air, said the functionary who looked after my uncle's business, "that the Princess will never get married."

"And why is that?"

"There are important reasons for that," replied the functionary, lowering his voice.

"Tell me, please be so kind," said I finally, addressing my aunt, "who on earth is this Princess Zizi?"

"She's related to the Gorodkovs. I think you must remember him: one of the Gorodkovs used to be around at your father's."

"I remember; a tall fellow, on the thin side, keen on greeting everyone."

"The Princess does indeed have some very strange qualities in her character. For example, hardly had her mother died when she, without even waiting a year, threw herself into gadding about everywhere – to theatres, to balls, lived in close harmony with her sister, then suddenly fell out with her and wanted to leave. But then she went on staying with her at home; she was on the point of marrying a very respectable man, and then suddenly for no apparent reason refused him. Then she started on some highly inappropriate legal case with her brother-in-law; then she wanted to go to a convent, and then she re-appeared in society. Well, in general, there really is a lot of strangeness in her. Last winter she travelled over to here and paid no visits to anyone – she didn't even come to see me… I am telling you, she really is very strange. She's quite a coquette – however, she has had really good marriage prospects but hasn't taken up any of them… There really is so much strangeness in her…"'

'My aunt's words failed to satisfy my curiosity. From what she said, I only learned that my aunt was cross with Princess Zizi for not paying her a visit. I was trying to compose for myself some sort of an understanding of this young lady, who had managed to arouse so many conflicting opinions about herself. Either, it seemed to me, she had to be just a rather mature Moscow maiden, reared on the novels of Madame Genlis, and with all the caprices of a convent girl; or, I thought, perhaps they called her strange for the same reasons that anyone, who is unlike everyone else, gets called an eccentric. Amid these meditations, I sat down at the table at which Maria Ivanovna, the impoverished widow who lived at auntie's as what they call "a companion", was as usual pouring the tea. She, like all "ladies' companions", was a great gossip, a past mistress of jam making, and a passionate enthusiast for good stories.

"You were asking your auntie about Princess Zizi," Maria Ivanovna said to me in a quiet voice, – "I didn't dare butt in, as everyone would get on to me, but no one knows her better than I do. I used to go to the old Princess' house to study dancing; that's where I got to know Princess Zinaida, and we are still friends and still in correspondence. Come and see us tomorrow before dinner and I will tell you in detail about this unfortunate girl's life history: she has been denigrated in society without any cause at all."'

With these words, my narrator pulled from the green briefcase a bundle of letters, took a deep breath, and shook his head,

'I keep these letters like something sacred,' he said, passing me one of them.

'The first one,' my friend continued. This was a letter from Princess Zizi to Maria Ivanovna. Glancing over it, I saw, to my surprise, that it had been written in a fairly correct Russian – and even just this, particularly for the time in question, was itself quite remarkable. The letter read as follows,

Moscow, 4th February, 18...
You have forgotten me, Masha, completely forgotten me. Two months have now already passed since your last letter. Have you really, away in your Kazan, found another good friend who has made you forget your poor Zizi? Write and tell me: what are you doing? Are you dancing? Uncle has sent us beautiful scarves from Paris – dark blue with white stripes for Lydia and a crimson one for me: but we don't get a chance to wear them. Besides, Mama wants me to wear the blue scarf and Lydia the crimson one. When I said that blue doesn't go with dark hair, Mama just got angry, as usual. We live just as before; Mama is always ill, is bored with everything, doesn't go out anywhere herself, and nobody comes to see us. God knows, we are pleased enough when old Rakitina comes over to see us, even if she only tells us what she has seen at Mass in her parish church. No one else comes to see us. So, you can see we are living very drearily. Of a morning, while Mama is praying, Lydia and I sit in the attic: she yawns away behind her canvas, as I do behind my book – as I, just as I used to, still steal books from Papa's library, it's my only comfort. Mama won't give me the key, though, saying that it's all men's books in this library, but

I've read the whole of Karamzin,[19] the whole history of the travels of the abbot Laporte,[20] and all of *The Herald of Europe*. I finally managed to get *Clarissa* off that shelf, if you remember, the one which had such strong wire along it – though I scratched my hand so badly that it really made me cry. Just the last volume of it I can't get at all: it has fallen behind a huge dictionary, and my hand just can't reach it – it's so annoying. Rakitina gave us several odd numbers of Russian journals, so you don't have the beginning or the end of anything: what makes these gents write 'continuation to follow' – I can't stand that phrase! But still, I did find there some fine poems by Zhukovsky[21] and that new poet, Pushkin! Everything of theirs goes straight to the heart and just sticks in the memory. I've written all their poems in my familiar (to you) notebook: it's now getting very fat. We go downstairs for dinner, and we sit with Mama and keep quiet until night-time. Whatever we might say, she just gets angry and complains continuously, about the weather, or about her health, and about other people. My sister and I have decided just to keep quiet and count chimneys from the window. But Mama just gets angry again, saying that we are abandoning her, avoiding her, that we are ungrateful, that – of course – it's boring to be with an old woman: and, you know, all her usual repetitions. God sees into my heart; I just ask one thing of him, that somehow he should cheer Mama up – but how to do that, he alone could know! In the summer it was rather more tolerable: at least we used to go off to the Simonov monastery – now, I could just cry. As for going away anywhere – don't even mention it! If we ask Mama to go out for a run in the carriage – she will sigh and groan, and that's the end of it. Goodbye, then, my dear Masha. Do write to me, for goodness' sake: at least you will

have a word to say about something. Your affectionate *Zizi*.
P.S. I completely forgot to tell you, but Lydia reminded me. Yesterday at Mass, Mama got very tired, and our servant wasn't anywhere near; but a young man noticed and rushed straight over, found a chair and sat Mama down; and she thanked him. It was some Mister Gorodkov or other; we had seen him in our parish a few times. It seems he's a neighbour of ours. Mama really took to him, and she – you won't believe this – seems to have invited him over. Yes, wait for it! – he's going to come over to our wilderness!…

'Number two,' said my friend, passing me another letter.

Moscow, 15th February
Thank you, Masha, for your letter. It cheered me up a lot. If you only knew – we laughed so much, just laughed, reading about the cavaliers of Kazan clomping their heels in the French quadrille; even Mama smiled. Generally now she is a bit happier. Vladimir Lukianovich Gorodkov has visited us – he's a really nice man. He really knew how to deal with Mummy! She was on at him about her lawsuits and he immediately got down to business, calmed Mummy down, and took from her a whole bundle of papers, promising to get busy with the law courts… He is a kind man! The good Lord must have sent him. Perhaps Mama will now be a bit happier – may God grant it! To celebrate, Mummy drove off with us to the city shops. Oh, how jolly it is there! Loads of people, carriages and noise… And what delights in the shops! I saw some absolutely new material: it's called *satin turque*. They do it double-faced – it's delightful! Mama bought the grey and orange tint for Lydia: that's now very fashionable. I'll send you a sample. And for me, Mama

bought the check taffeta. You must advise me on the fashion I should have it made up in! I want the bodice to be with slits, with epaulettes on the shoulders, a little sash jutting out, and a falbala – a hem that's let out sewn all around. Don't you think that would be wonderful? …

'This whole letter,' I said to my friend, 'is just about rags and finery. What's interesting in that? And, I must confess, up to now I don't see any of the unusual qualities you were talking so much about. I can see that her mother is a depressed old fool who torments her daughters quite senselessly, and the daughters just want to get dressed up and get married: we can see this every day…'

'Number three,' my friend announced icily.

Moscow, 3rd April

You don't know what's going on with us, Masha. Just imagine that I am really in prison – yes, in prison: I don't go down from the attic. But wait a bit, I must tell you everything in the right order. All this time Gorodkov has not stopped visiting us; Mama is out of her mind with him. He fixed all Mummy's business affairs, he managed to reassure her that they were not anything like as bad as she thought they were, although they did require attention… It's true: this man has behaved better than a relative. We have got so used to him that when he misses seeing us for a day, then we start wondering whether he is ill, and Mama sends off to enquire about his health. In short, … But listen; for some time now, as soon as Vladimir Lukianovich arrives, Mama will start saying that she thinks I am not quite myself, or will find something or other, some pretext, to send me up to the attic. For a long time I couldn't make out why, but now

I have guessed: Mama imagines that Vladimir Lukianovich is making eyes at us, and she wants Lydia, as the elder, to get married before me. Now she has simply forbidden me to come down from the attic, and persuades Vladimir Lukianovich that I am unwell. But I think that this is all groundless. It's true, he's very courteous with us, but that's with both of us. He brings Lydia designs for craft canvases; and he brings me books. He doesn't talk to either one of us any more than the other, and he really doesn't dream of Mama's ideas. This will have to end somehow or other! But meanwhile, it's very tiresome for me to have to keep sitting in the attic, especially when Vladimir Lukianovich is down below: he is so cheerful, so amusing – he always knows how to keep you interested. He's also a man of letters, it seems, but I haven't been able to test this out thoroughly, though I would really like to talk to him about literature, about Zhukovsky, about Pushkin, but I'm afraid that he might see me as a pedant – and anyway, now there's no chance. I'm so annoyed, that I can't read a thing. My only concern is to hang about on the staircase listening in to what they are saying below. It does have its funny side! If only it would all somehow finish soon! I would very much like him to marry Lydia: then we will really be able to live a bit more happily. I shall be able to go about with her to dances and parties, because she will then be a *lady*. I shall definitely ask her to take me to the bookshop: I've never yet been in the bookshop. Vladimir Lukianovich really knows writers, I shall be able to meet some real author, perhaps Zhukovsky – what a man he must be...! But meanwhile I am still stuck in the attic! Goodbye, my dear Masha. Do write to your poor recluse.

Zizi

'Number four.'

Masha! My fate has been decided: I am in love, Masha, I am madly in love! I have been wanting to hide this, both from you and from myself, but I can no longer confine this secret to my soul... I fell in love with him from the first minute I met him, and I cannot live without him... If you could only see him, you would understand completely. He is the combination of all perfections: really handsome, with eyes on fire; and his heart, his kind, beautiful heart, his mild and quiet conversation, his gentle manner... I'm out of my mind, Masha. I am ashamed of myself; I'm ready to run after him to the end of the world – and I can't even see him. The whole day I spend pinned to the window in my accursed attic, just to catch the clattering sounds of his droshky: I would recognise these among thousands. I catch the sound, and my blood runs cold in my veins, my heart beats, I just start shaking and I am completely on fire, my eyes go dark and my head goes round – my strength all goes. When he drives away, I rush downstairs, I look for the chair which he has been sitting on, the table which he would have gone up to, and the doors he will have gone out through. I am ready to kiss all of these, and at this point torment strikes. Lydia, that cold Lydia, relates what he said, jokes, laughs about him, and I ... I am jealous, I am ready to tear Lydia to pieces... Oh, what is Mama doing to me? Why did she allow me to see him at the start? Why does she now forbid me? ... He is not indifferent to me: he always asks after me, asks what the doctor has said. *He* is being pitilessly deceived... What if my false illness is upsetting him? And I have to keep quiet, hide everything that's in my heart, in front of my sister and in front of Mummy...! Sometimes

I am ready to come out with everything, but as soon as I see her severe expression, my tongue stays glued; and she just gets angry or says that she won't hear a word about my depression. But, at least, up until now she hasn't got her way at all. Up until now he has made no declarations. I am waiting for this, as one would await a death sentence... Oh, do have pity for your

Zizi!

'Number five.'

Cry, Masha, and pray for me! I need your prayers: myself, I cannot pray – you understand, everything's finished... He made his declaration, he is betrothed ... to Lydia. This was yesterday; I lay unconscious in bed at that time, and Mama really did send for the doctor. What can a doctor do? Everything has finished for me! My world now is the coffin; my hope is death. Oh, Lydia, lucky Lydia! And what was it he found in her? And with her it's as if nothing had happened! Will she make him happy? She's as cold as ice. For her, getting married is like drinking a glass of water. She lies in bed asleep, just as before. She sews away at her canvas in the same way. She eats away through dinner just the same, and she's surprised that I should wander about like crazy the whole night, that a morsel of food doesn't pass my lips, and that I should have thrown all my books on to the floor. I often want to believe that all this is just a bad dream. I often think that it will just pass, just disappear. I try my utmost to wake up – it's a futile dream! Lydia comes up to me to show off her wedding dress. She asks me to help her lay a frill. She laughs and guffaws, with no conception of her happiness... Is she to be the wife of this angel...? The ungrateful, unfaithful, treacherous man – he doesn't realise what he has lost in me. I would have consoled him every minute of his life; I would have watched over him at night; I would have made up to him all day long; I would have made him laugh when he was bored; I would have pampered him like a child... But I can't write any longer. My tears are falling on the paper, my fingers are shaking, and the whole room is spinning round me. Pray, do pray for me, Masha!

'Princess Zinaida's letters, Maria Ivanovna told me, concerned and frightened her. She was aware of the Princess' fiery imagination, knowing that, accustomed to the strict treatment of her mother, to the complete absence of any sort of kindness, Zinaida was bound to take any affectionate word to be the unquestionable sign of a generous heart. She knew that, having lived for an age within four walls, Zinaida was bound to fall for the first man who would appear before her eyes. But perhaps this man was unworthy of her trust, perhaps he would want to take advantage of her inexperience... All this struck Maria Ivanovna in the worst possible light. "Circumstances forced me," she said, "to look more carefully into people from my early years, to assess them more strictly; in short, I was older than Zizi not only in years, but in life as well."

But what was there for her to do? Writing to console her friend would be an impossible task. The people in whose house Maria Ivanovna was living were intending to make a trip to Moscow. She asked them to take her with them.

Having arrived here, she immediately learned two pieces of news: of Princess Lydia's wedding and the death of her mother. Maria Ivanovna found Princess Zinaida at her sister's home. The second blow, apparently, had lessened the effect of the first one. Truly, the Princess had lost a lot of weight, but she was still very attractive. She was very sad, but calmer than Maria Ivanovna had expected. Zinaida said little about Lydia, or about her husband, but recounted in detail the last days of her mother: the way she had bidden her children farewell, the way she had asked their forgiveness, how she had asked them to remember her, and how she had entreated Zinaida never to leave her sister.

"You know," said the old lady when left alone with Zinaida, "that although you are the younger, I have greater hopes in you. You know that Lydia hasn't got a brain in her head. I can see now: she won't be capable of settling down properly with her husband; neither will she know how to bring up children, or manage the estates. Although I am glad that I got her married, I really do fear for her. If the good Lord had only lengthened my life, I could have been able to support her, restrain her, exhort her. But the Lord didn't want it that way – so let that be his sacred will! So I am entrusting my task to you, Zinaida: look after her, like you would a child, don't let her waste lots of money, avert her from quarrels with her husband – she is a bit unbalanced, as you know. Love her children, love her, love..."

Zinaida couldn't bring herself to say whom. But, I repeat, she was quite calm: she understood the magnitude of her sacrifice, and an involuntary feeling of self-satisfaction crept into her heart. Life for her would not be without a purpose.

Maria Ivanovna got to know Gorodkov as well. Looking at him, she understood that no woman could be indifferent towards him. He was a fine young man, dressed in a clean, dandified fashion, had a cheerful, even humorous disposition, treated Lydia without excessive endearment, but with great courtesy, and Zinaida – with the greatest possible signs of respect. Maria Ivanovna dined together with them in Zinaida's rooms – she, not having completely recovered her health, had been allotted her own half of the premises. The whole time at table, Vladimir Lukianovich was very pleasant and talkative, reading out several charade instructions that he was intending to send to *The Herald of Europe* and which, as Maria Ivanovna noted, had been written in verse and were very intricate. Then he told of his acquaintance with various authors and other famous people. All his anecdotes were quite fascinating, so much so that as Maria Ivanovna admitted, the time flew and several times Zinaida herself could not help smiling. After dinner he bade them farewell, saying that he had to go out to attend to some business affairs which, after the old Princess, had remained in great disorder. Thus was the impression Gorodkov had created, even on the sensible Maria Ivanovna. Soon after this, she had to travel back again to Kazan with her household. About a year went by. In the course of that time she received several letters from Zinaida which, however, contained nothing that was new to her. But this is one that is rather more remarkable,'

> I am rushing to tell you, my dear Masha, that God has favoured Lydia with a daughter: yesterday, at around midday, she gave birth very successfully. Her daughter has been called Praskov'ia, in Mama's honour. And so, our family has become larger by one more person. What is there to tell you about me? My fever has gone; I don't spend my nights in constant tears, but I can admit to you that I often do feel such a heavy-heartedness that it's impossible to describe. If I were a thousand versts the other side of Moscow, then perhaps I could forget about everything. But to have the happiness which will never belong to me continually before my eyes – that is what's awful. To conceal my feelings from

everyone, from my sister, from myself, from *him* – that's what is intolerable. My one consolation is prayer. That's when I remember Mama's words, the promise I gave, and I calm down. I am only now beginning to grasp the whole truth of her words. I can write openly to you: without me, Lydia would be in a desperate mess. I could never imagine how hopeless she would be as mistress of the house. She doesn't know the value of anything; she gives instructions and then will forget, and order quite the opposite. The servants don't know what to do; now they've got used to asking me, and I, taking advantage of Lydia's forgetfulness, change her instructions without any permission. This is all of no matter to her – it's even greatly to her liking that she doesn't have to mess about with any of this at all – she can sleep for half the day and go round the shops for the other half. And there too I have to restrain her, for, like a child, she's ready to buy everything that appears before her eyes. In this way, I often prevent domestic flare-ups, which would otherwise be unavoidable, for *he* is an efficient master, keen on everything being in order. Often in the long winter evenings he and I would talk away about our household matters; he would report to me on the running of our mutual estate; I would tell him all about my household instructions and Lydia would doze. She has nothing to do with any of it; and, at such times, I feel as though I am the real mistress in the house, that I – I'm afraid to come out with it – am his wife... But the clock sounds, he and Lydia get up, and I, with my heart clenched, drag myself off to my solitary cell and fling myself into my cold bed... But away with these thoughts! I don't want to grumble to Providence; it has created me for an agonising, daily, long-drawn-out suffering. But it has given me consolation, too: it has accorded me the means of furthering the happiness of a noble and honourable man, the means of preserving the composure of his wonderful soul, although he has no suspicion of this. I look upon myself as a creature of sacrifice, who has brought him happiness, a pure and disinterested sacrifice – and this notion elevates my soul. I am almost happy, my daydreams are half accomplished. With each day, I try to become more worthy of my duty. You may believe it, that as soon as Lydia became pregnant, I took to reading books on upbringing. These books, perhaps, at another time would have seemed tedious to me, but they insusceptibly broadened my range of thought. I see a lot of things more clearly and many new feelings have sprung up in my soul; sometimes, in forgetfulness, I feel as though the calling of mother has been entrusted to me, that I could say to him '*our child*'. Oh, and then my heart beats wildly, the blood rises to my head, and strange things go through my mind, the sort of thoughts with which I can frighten myself, so I jump up and throw myself on to my knees before the icon. Yesterday, when I was praying with tears in my eyes, the first cry rang out from Lydia's infant… *his* infant. What went through me at that moment, I really haven't the strength to tell you. It was both an inexpressible sorrow and an inexpressible joy; both hell and paradise. I both wept and laughed, I prayed and I cursed. I felt a trembling in every nerve, my ears were ringing and my breath was caught; I was ready to rush to the infant, to smother her with kisses and to tear her to pieces… Such a condition could not last long: I collapsed unconscious. When I came to, all my depravity had quietened down; Mama's image was floating in front of me. I could see before me just his child and my duty. And Lydia, Lydia … she is still weak, but is already

> complaining just about one thing – that she won't be able to go out anywhere for the duration of several weeks. How happy she is, or, perhaps I had better say, how unhappy…!

'Within a certain time after this letter, there set out from Kazan to work in Moscow a young man, who was a relation of Maria Ivanovna's people. He was a person not without means, youthful, not bad looking, something of a poet, and possessed of a completely romantic novelistic character. He asked Maria Ivanovna for letters of introduction to her Moscow acquaintances. As she glanced at him, a sort of vague idea ran through the mind of Zinaida's friend: she gave him a note to the Princess, with the task of handing it to her personally – only not to fall in love. "Who knows," Maria Ivanovna thought, "this young man might appeal to her; she's young, her feelings are spirited; and so, perhaps, a fortunate change might take place within her, and she might escape from her excruciating situation." The letter which Maria Ivanovna received from Zizi soon afterwards convinced her that she had done the right thing. This is it,'

> Lydia has completely recovered. We have already started going out. Often I would like to stay at home with my Pashenka, who is growing prettier by the day, loves me more than she does her wet-nurse, and holds her little hands out to me. But Lydia can't be left to go out alone: as I have told you, she is a real child; she loves the fashions, but she can never understand which things suit her and which things don't. It costs me enormous effort sometimes to persuade her not to raise her waistline so high that it would disfigure her completely. In society she drives me utterly to despair. She can be so delighted with music, at a ball, or with her

own attire, that she cannot conceal her enjoyment. At times, forgetting herself completely, she can guffaw across the whole hall so that everyone turns round. Especially in the theatre, I have to keep tugging at her sleeve, so that she won't say something indecent to the young people who crowd up to us in our box. Vladimir Lukianovich seems to notice all this and indirectly gives me to feel his gratitude. Yesterday, while Lydia was trying on a new dress in the bathroom for the tenth time, I was sitting in the bedroom, rocking Pasha in my arms. He came up to me and looked at me pensively for some time. I became unwittingly embarrassed; in order to bring this odd situation to an end, I asked him what he was thinking about. 'About you,' he replied gently, 'perhaps you don't know how I often think about you, Zinaida.' At this point he came up to me, took me by the hand and, with a melancholy glance, pressed it. I started to quiver; this was the first time ever that he had touched my hand so tenderly… Not knowing what to reply, I turned to caressing Pashenka, and he flung himself into an armchair standing in the other corner. I don't know whether he noticed my confusion, or whether this was precisely what his words intended, but he continued with particular expression, attaching weight to each word, 'I should like to arrange your estate, so as to separate off for you your portion, so that you should have your own independent property.'

'But what for?' I asked. 'Can it really not remain under your management?'

'But you could get married,' he answered, looking at me intently, 'so everything needs to be in order.'

'Oh, never!' I cried, quite forgetting myself, and then, thinking better of it, I started to come out with a few insignificant words so as to explain my thinking: but these just revealed my embarrassment all the more.

'You girls are all the same like that: how can you possibly answer for yourself, for that day?' he continued with the very same expression and not taking his eyes off me. I made no reply and he went on, 'Yes, this will absolutely have to be done; I am now trying to conclude the lawsuit over the forest land, and then our hands will be untied.'

At this point, Lydia walked in, turning round and showing off her dress; our conversation ceased. Get married... Up until now, this thought had never yet entered my head; to get married to someone else... Lord, have mercy on me!

Letter from Princess Zizi to Maria Ivanovna, a month later

Thank you, my dear Masha, for your letter, which your Kazan acquaintance Radetsky brought me. I couldn't reply to you right away, because Pasha was sick, and Lydia as well. She is pregnant again and, despite all the admonitions of the doctors, she still dances away – as they might say, she never leaves the floor. Your acquaintance is very pleasant – except, seemingly, that he's of an over-romantic character. He looks at me with such strange eyes that it just strikes me as funny – or is that just the fashion where you are, in Kazan? It seems to me that he hasn't gone down all that well either with Vladimir Lukianovich. He is civil with him and polite enough, as he would be, but – between ourselves – Vladimir Lukianovich jokingly calls him 'the wishy-washy' and, I admit to you, I have to agree. Vladimir Lukianovich is very concerned about our lawsuit with the exchequer; however solid his character, this business visibly worries him. Often, when Lydia is still at some ball, he will drive home before her and sit all night at his papers. I know this only too well, as he will always call in to see me. Nowadays, thank God, he doesn't insist any more that I should go out with Lydia and he seems to be glad that I should stay at home, because Pashenka is constantly ill, whereas Lydia cannot get by without her dancing. As for me, nothing about a ball interests me and I am quite happy enough just to get to my room. Goodbye.

'This letter, notwithstanding its dispassionate tone, really alarmed Maria Ivanovna. There was something unsaid in it; the Princess was keeping something from her. Radetsky's letter will explain to you this enigma – to a certain extent.'

Letter from Radetsky to Maria Ivanovna

My dear Madam, Maria Ivanovna! What a good task you charged me with. I fulfilled it to the letter: I have fallen in love with your splendid friend to an extent I would never have expected – that is to say head over heels. How this happened, I am not going to tell you, because I don't know myself. The thing is, my fate is decided; I feel that I just cannot live without Princess Zinaida. You began it, so must bring it to a conclusion. You were the cause of my acquaintance with her, so you must help me. You will perhaps ask me whether she has taken a liking to me – that's the whole thing... Princess Zinaida's feelings towards me are impenetrable. In my conversations with her I have noticed her fine, educated mind; but as to what is concealed behind that mind – that is an unknown quantity. She seems to me to belong to that category of women who are blessed by nature with a tender heart, but in whom pride hinders real feeling.

Feeling seems to them to be a weakness, something humiliating. They are afraid to bare their heart; they try to protect it with any kind of trumpery, in order to escape from the piercing eyes of a man. Perhaps I am mistaken, but that's how Princess Zinaida appears to me. What this stems from, from the manner of her upbringing, or from a flawed disposition, I don't know, except that I don't really understand my princess. I have not yet spoken to her of my love, so much do I fear this girl. Just one word from her would signify my life or death, and it could be that her pride or excessive modesty would force her to utter a dreadful 'no', even should her heart be contradicting that very word. You know Princess Zinaida better than I do: coach me in what I should do, what I should say, how I should look at her. With just one glance she can reduce me to a quiver, and the words which break from my soul just die on my tongue. Tell me, wouldn't it be better if you were to write to her, if you were, from the side, to try to elicit her thoughts about me. It is not possible that she doesn't realise what's happening with me. Does she really think that I endeavour to drive over to their house as often as I do just for the pleasure of listening to the cold civilities of her brother-in-law, his ramblings about literature published in *The Herald of Europe*, intermingled with stories about grand dinners? Above all, she must realise that I, to put it in society's terms, have the right to offer her my hand. As you know, I am not a pauper, we are of similar age, I have a respectable rank, and future prospects. All that is, of course, a lot of nonsense, but I mention it at all only for the reason that it should all have drawn the Princess' attention to me one way or another – but no such thing seems to be the case. It's already into the third month that I have been going to their house and the Princess treats me as she did at our first meeting: not a sign of displeasure, not a sign of friendliness; as before, she's gentle enough with me, amiable and cold. What is the explanation? From another viewpoint, is her present maidenly life really so precious to her? She doesn't have her mother, she is living in effect in someone else's home, the whole day she nurses another's child, and occupies the role of some sort of governess, or even housekeeper. She is a woman with a good brain and widely read, with a fiery imagination! … I don't understand it. For God's sake, explain all this to me, if you can, and don't delay your reply. Every minute is for me an age of suffering.

Radetsky

'Receiving this letter, Maria Ivanovna, as may be obvious, fell into quite a quandary. What, indeed, was she to reply to Radetsky? To entrust him with Zinaida's secret would be an impossible thing to do. Writing to Zinaida, describing to her all Radetsky's virtues: that would be useless. She could anticipate some success to come from his young eyes, from his intelligence, and from his kindness – but not from letters from her. As far as I can guess, her own self-regard must have whispered to Maria Ivanovna that she was interfering to no purpose in this affair. And so she decided upon what indecisive people usually decide – that is to do nothing, not to reply to Radetsky, and to leave the denouement to his own wits, in his own time. But two postal delivery days had not passed before Maria Ivanovna received a new letter from Radetsky. This is it,'

You are not replying to me, may God be your judge! Not to answer me at the very minute when my whole life is a succession of unbroken torments…! Not only have my affairs not advanced, but they have even regressed, because I have quarrelled with Gorodkov, and I don't myself even know how. This is how it came about. They had a soirée; everyone was seated at cards; there were only three non-participants: the mistress of the house, the Princess and I. I sat down at the table by the divan, on which the two sisters were sitting. I was very glad to have this opportunity of talking to her, in effect in private, as the mistress of the house didn't really count: either she kept quiet, not following our conversation, or she laughed loudly for no reason, or else she would just leap up from her seat. The Princess was even more pensive than usual.

'You don't play?' said the Princess, raising her shining, dark eyes to me.

'Even without cards,' I replied, 'there are enough torments in this world. I don't know why people have to contrive new means of self-harassment when there are more than enough old ones.'

The Princess smiled; but, if I'm not mistaken, there was something sad in her smile.

'Please be so kind,' she said in a derisive tone, 'as to stop putting on that act. I know that these days it's very much in fashion for young people to play the martyr's role, to keep on about the passing of youth, about lost hopes. You can't even imagine how hilarious all this is.'

These words cut me to the quick.

'Would you really,' I asked, 'from there being some people who pretend to be ill, be of a disposition to laugh, if you were to see someone on their deathbed?'

'No, but I would send for a doctor.'

'And if the doctor didn't want to come?'

'I would send for another one.'

'Do you really think that changing doctors is that easy?'

I don't know what in this insignificant question made the Princess so pensive, or at least, that's how it seemed to me, but she swiftly changed the conversation.

'Will you be staying much longer in Moscow?'

'I don't know; I am not my own master in …'

'Well, who is, then?' the Princess asked ingenuously.

'I have a responsibility to one of those speeches which make you laugh so much.'

'Again! How droll you young men are now!'

'Just as droll as all young men have been, since the world was created, in particular circumstances.'

'Without joking, I think that for the greater part you yourselves do not know what you want. A few words wander about in your heads, a few verses learned by heart, out of which you draw up something resembling life, and then you convince yourselves that this life is torturing you.'

'Do you really, Princess, think like that about everyone, without exception?'

'Oh, no!' she said in her usual manner of speaking. 'But I do of many,' she added calmly. 'So little is required for happiness in life, but this is not understood by very many: they all chase after the impossible, like children after a shadow, and then they complain that they can't catch it.'

'You quite rightly stated that little is required for happiness, but similarly little is required for suffering. Sometimes in these things a person himself will be responsible, an impure conscience, mercenary feelings, a depraved or forbidden passion – of this, there is nothing to be said. But it can happen that in someone's soul there burns a pure, sacred feeling, that one feels in oneself a capacity to dedicate the whole of one's life, for instance to a woman, and that this is responded to with coldness, with scorn…'

My words manifestly made an impression on the Princess: she was in a state of agitation, at first blushing and then turning pale; her chest rose considerably. I could see the reaction my words produced, and tried to take advantage of that rare moment that had awakened feeling in the Princess, to express in words all that had caused the turmoil in my own soul. But the master of the house came over to me.

'Do me the favour,' he said to me cordially, 'of taking my place at Boston for a minute; I need to go and give some orders in the house…'

At this minute, I was ready to throw him out of the window.

'I don't play… I don't know how to play it!' I said with visible annoyance.

'But just for a minute, only a minute, you could hold the cards in your hand,' he answered, smiling. 'But still, just as you please; I don't want to force you to do me a favour. Excuse me for troubling you,' he added coolly.

I collected myself, and wanted to ask him for the cards, but he was already greeting a newly arrived guest, who eagerly accepted his same proposal. I looked round and the Princess had disappeared: I remained, cheek-by-jowl, with the mistress of the house.

'What was the matter with the Princess?' I asked her.

'She suddenly felt sleepy,' replied Lydia and guffawed for all she was worth.

What on earth was I going to converse with her about? I was upset, enraged, and in no condition to intersperse the empty with the vacuous. Taking advantage of the first moment when Lydia Petrovna jumped up, as was her wont, I ran out of the house like a madman.

You can imagine what was going through me at that time! To have been awaiting this minute of cherished paradise for days on end; to be interrupted just when, perhaps, her heart was beginning to be open to feeling, and then to remain with the enigma unresolved, and without having fully poured out my heart… it's terrible!

The whole night I couldn't get to sleep and early in the morning I drove over to Gorodkov, wanting to apologise for my discourtesy; I was not admitted. The next day, the same thing; the day after that, again the same. I inquired about the health of the entire household, each in turn, and the servants replied that all, the Lord be praised, were well, and had been pleased to leave on a drive out. But this wasn't true: the carriages were standing in the courtyard, and consequently the masters were at home. It simply meant that they didn't wish to receive me. I didn't know what to do. I had just decided to write to Gorodkov and explain everything openly to him, but the fear of exposing my fate to the written word, without having prepared the Princess for my declaration, held me back. In the evening I encountered Gorodkov at the house of mutual acquaintances and reluctantly went up to him, about to begin apologising for my discourtesy. He cut short my speech, with his customary smile, saying, 'Oh! For goodness' sake, how is this possible! Do we have anything to speak about? Do me the favour of not troubling yourself!' – and so on, and so forth; and, in so doing, he turned to someone else. To start speaking to him again was, at that moment, beyond my powers. But all the same, I decided to drive over to him the next day, but again I wasn't admitted. I was completely in despair; every day

I went to the post, to see whether there might be a letter from you, in case one had been mislaid, but in vain!

For goodness' sake, don't delay in replying, don't torment me. You best know the family relationships in this house: explain to me what all this means. Could Zinaida's brother-in-law really get so angry with me for a thing that is so usual in society? There must be hidden here some secret or other, which I have been racking my brains over to no avail. I cannot conceal from you that Mr Gorodkov's behaviour seems most strange to me. He enjoys the finest reputation in society; he is received into the best houses; he is very amiable in his manner, but I never took to him the first time I met him – and do you know why? He sidles into the room; he always somehow creeps around people. I don't want to censure him without cause; such involuntary deportment could stem from some low feeling deep down within him; it could equally stem from excessive modesty or bashfulness. But, as you may please: he is certainly something over polite, over amiable, over compliant. Having achieved a certain lifestyle, and a certain what they call 'aplomb', he is still everywhere on the lookout for something, agreeing with what he shouldn't be agreeing with, smiling at someone he cannot stand. All of this, if you like, oversteps the limits of normal good manners and crosses the line at which courtesy becomes indistinguishable from pretence and colourlessness of character – perhaps from secret and serious misdemeanours. I cannot comprehend the existence of a man who never disagrees with anyone, any more than I can a man who argues just for the sake of arguing. In short, there is something unintelligible in this Gorodkov. In the present-day social world, when the art of hypocrisy has fitted into the rules of education somewhere in between grammar and morality, it is difficult to fathom a man. You have to know his entire history from the cradle in order to formulate for yourself any sort of a conception. I started to recall as much as I knew about Gorodkov: that he had always been in the service, didn't take bribes, that he was inclined to the classics, played Boston very well, writes charades, and that's about all. But when I look at his head, flooding into the collar of his tailcoat, at that barely perceptible wrinkle beside the eyes beneath his temples, at his ruddy, eternally smiling face, a hidden voice tells me that all this is all a mask, not what is really within him. For the love of God, tell me everything you know about him and what you conclude from this most recent behaviour of his, but most of all, write about Zinaida. Have you been writing to her? What did she reply? For the love of God, don't let me waste away in a slow death. She has no relatives; you are my only hope. I really don't know now what I am in a state to decide upon.

'Poor Maria Ivanovna, on receipt of this letter, was thrown into considerable confusion. While she was preparing herself to reply to it, this following new letter arrived,'

I rush to let you know that my fate has been decided. I am happy, so happy, that I can't express it: *Princess Zinaida has agreed to marry me!* I am crying from happiness, like a child. Our declaration of love was very strange. This is how it came about: judge for yourself.

Receiving ceaseless refusals at the house, I, like a stereotyped lover, was wandering around beneath the windows of my beloved, but all in vain. The Princess didn't leave the courtyard and didn't approach the window. The domestics, from whom I enquired about her health, looked at me mockingly. The displeasure of the gentry passed over to the servants, as usually happens, without any recognition on their part: the master looks askance and they do likewise. But, fortunately, there does exist in this world the mighty fifty-kopeck piece, by means of which doors do open and by dint of which the mute can become talkative. In this way did I learn that the Princess was at church – so there I hurried off. Inside the church, it was dark; with difficulty, in a distant corner behind a pillar, I recognised the Princess. There were few parishioners there; she, probably thinking that no attention would be paid to her, was on her knees, praying ardently and weeping bitterly. I didn't want to disturb her and stood where she wouldn't notice me. What did these tears mean? Were they a matter purely of piety, or of some secret sorrow? Whichever might be the case, it seemed to me that it was now my duty to speak with the Princess. I waited for the conclusion of the service and, when the Princess was going out with the rest into the church porch, I went up to her. Glancing at her in the dim light of a candle, burning by an image, I became alarmed: her eyes were red, her cheeks were shrunken, her face bore the imprint of a severe inner suffering.

'Princess!' I exclaimed, 'it's essential that I say a few words to you.'

In the first instant, she seemed to be alarmed and to want to get away from me; but then, reconsidering a little, she stopped and replied,

'Go on, then. I am listening.'

We went out into the portico. She sent the lackey who was accompanying her over to the church railings. Never yet had she seemed to me so beautiful... It was a quiet evening; the sun's last crimson rays lit up her attractive and noble face, around which, from under a straw hat, wound down to the shoulders in some disorder her dark, fine curls.

'Princess!' I said in a firm voice, 'you are unhappy!'

In a single instant, across her face, so dispirited by misfortune, there flashed her customary sense of pride.

'Who gives you the right,' she replied, 'to be calling me to account?'

'What gives me such a right is that feeling which you have inspired in me, and the oath taken by me before God, to whom we have together just been praying, to dedicate my life to you until my last breath. In my present position, I have to speak directly and decisively.'

The Princess became thoughtful; bitter tears poured from her eyes. Her proud expression disappeared; for a moment, in a flash crossing her face, I could see before me a weak and tormented woman...

Suddenly, she took me by the hand,

'Tell me, you are not deceiving me...?'

'Oh, Princess...!'

'You would be prepared to marry me, were I to agree?'

'We really cannot talk here. Don't ask me about anything... In just a few hours, I shall send you a letter, to the house...'

I wanted to kiss her hand, but, pulling back, she made off over to the railings. I wanted to follow her, but she signalled to me that I should leave her alone. I returned home deep in thought. Much as I might rejoice at my hopes for happiness, so swift and unexpected a fulfilment of my wishes did alarm me. In the Princess' behaviour, as before, there was something strange and indescribable: I was lost in conjecture. Not half an hour had passed, when I received from her the following note: 'I am ready to give you my hand and put my trust in you as an honest man; but particular circumstances force me to desire that our marriage should take place as soon as possible. My one condition is that you must not ask me about the reason for such a strange request; don't ask me about anything; entrust yourself unconditionally to my conscience... One day, you will know everything.'

I replied to this note, saying that I have faith in her noble heart, that I shall not be asking her about anything, and that I hope, as soon as tomorrow, to arrange everything for our wedding.

So that is what has happened to me. Even though I still haven't received any reply from you, I don't have anyone here with whom I can share my curious happiness. I am writing to you at night; my mental excitement prevents me from closing my eyes. At first light, I'll be off to see about arranging everything for the wedding ceremony. I doubt whether anyone has managed to get himself married quite like this!

'In the following post, Maria Ivanovna received the following letter from the young man,'

It's all finished. My fate has been settled. This is the new note written to me by Princess Zinaida, 'Forgive me, do not curse me; just consider me crazy, if you wish. No, my noble young man, I cannot be your wife! I don't want to deceive you: I cannot love you. Try to find another woman, one who would be worthy of you. I know that there's no justification for my action, but in your heart I should at least find forgiveness. Don't ask for elaboration from an unfortunate victim of fate; don't try to find out my secret; forget, just forget me!'

I have nothing to add to this letter: you can just imagine my condition. For goodness' sake, write and tell me what you understand in all this. Even if I cannot be happy myself, this doesn't prevent me from sacrificing my life, if needs be, in order to save a poor girl from the inexplicable, but actual, intrigues, which perhaps surround her. The penetration of these intrigues I consider my sacred duty. I am already beginning to suspect some of them, but perhaps this is all just fancy... My ideas do not have any sound basis. The net in which the Princess is caught is plaited so artfully that it escapes the most perspicacious gaze. In my mortal grief, I don't even have the strength to act. My thoughts are confused, one just destroys another, and after a tense struggle, I find only that I am suffering, suffering terribly, and I don't see any end to my suffering. Write to me at least a couple of words; perhaps they may direct me towards the discovery of what I am being tormented by.

'This time Maria Ivanovna decided to reply to the young man. It seems that she replied to him in empty phrases and assurances that she herself found Zinaida's conduct absolutely incomprehensible. Her good will towards the friend of her childhood prevented her from revealing her awful secret, but in the mean time she wrote a letter to her in which, so I was told, in the strongest possible terms to which she could lay her pen, she reproached her for her behaviour. She alluded to being able to guess the reason for it and, for the first time in her life, dared to tell the Princess how iniquitous her fervour was. Princess Zinaida's reply was a rather curious one. Here it is,'

If anyone else, other than you, had reproached me, I would have paid no attention to such reproaches. But you, you know my position, you know all the torments of my heart, the whole long struggle I have had with myself, which has lasted not a day, not two days, but years – and you can reproach me! Yes. My behaviour with Radetsky might be inexcusable in the eyes of society, but not in your eyes. I pity the young man, but what can be done? At a moment of sorrow and despair I thought that, by marriage to him, I could stifle what is going on in my heart and what I do not dare talk about. But when I read in his note that tomorrow I have to appear with him before the altar, all my resolve left me. Deceive someone, swear to him eternal love, when I... no, this was impossible! I decided that it was better to sacrifice myself, to be taken for a scatter-brained, crazy... My fate is decided. I shall never belong to anyone; and when neither Lydia, nor her children, will have need of me any more, then the nunnery will hide this unfortunate woman – if not from her own sufferings, then at least from society's understandings. But then again, if I am guilty before Radetsky of a lot of things, then he too inflicted the cruellest insult upon me, something which only his jealousy could contrive. Radetsky is a man without a heart. But what he says about me, an insulting suspicion which he could not conceal – all that, I can forgive him. But, in his indignation against me, he is trying to vent his bile on everything around me. Just imagine, he took the liberty of writing to me that he had delved into my life, that he could guess who was *standing in the way* of my marrying him. He took the liberty too of warning me, and accusing of all sorts of self-serving designs – whom do you think? – *him*, that angel of kindness and disinterestedness... Because the straightforwardness of his mind, and of his heart, do not allow him romantic ravings; because he sees life more clearly than other people and he hides his lofty sentiments deep in his heart – your Childe Harold *manqué* considers *him* capable of mean and self-serving designs…! This letter, I must confess, has even consoled me: I appear to myself less guilty before Radetsky than previously; for only he who is himself capable of such shabby reckoning could contrive such a fabrication – and against whom…? Where is justice in this world? A young man falls in love, his intentions are not successful, and he considers he has the right to slander a hero of virtue, an unfortunate… as unfortunate, perhaps, as I am myself?

'In this letter too, as you may see, there is much left unsaid. The Princess concealed a lot from her *confidante*.

'However, Maria Ivanovna did subsequently learn of everything that had taken place in the intervals between these letters.

'After a while, when the Princess began to go out and about rather more, Gorodkov became perceptibly uneasy. He found various pretexts to restrain his wife from such outings. He would often start talking about family happiness, about the costs which such outings entail, and about the solemn duty of the head of the family to try to moderate his expenses, in order to leave more to the children. But these words touched only Princess Zinaida – as for Lydia, she was oblivious to them. Whatever may have been the limits of her comprehension, Lydia nevertheless remained a granddaughter of Eve and still knew with an inscrutable artistry how to organise certain household circumstances, so as to ensure that outings became essential. Her husband even, for all his perspicacity, involuntarily admired his wife's sway. An unexpected visit would crop up, which really had to be paid, and this visit would lead to some new acquaintanceship. Or an invitation would arrive to such and such a house, where he could meet up with some particularly useful man. All this would be arranged as though by accident, whereas it was all really the ingenious Lydia's doing. For this purpose she availed herself of cunning and initiative; with the young men with whom she flirted, she established an indubitable plot against her husband. With their help, she worked on people's aunties, grandmothers – in short, on all *invitation senders* – and, thanks to this tactic, there was no shortage of outings. Not succeeding in this matter, Vladimir Lukianovich turned to another route: for a few days before a trip away, he would begin worrying about his daughter's health. "What do you think it is, Zinaida Petrovna?" he would say, "Pasha doesn't seem very well: just look, her eyes look a bit drowsy and she's not eating very much." Zinaida would get anxious and send for the doctor; the doctor would advise giving the infant some German powder or other: then the child would really get ill and the Princess, of course, would stay at home. Radetsky's appearance in the house troubled the perspicacious Vladimir Lukianovich considerably. In general, he could not bear people who were not quite his own stamp, those who didn't read exactly what he read, didn't say the same things he said, were not carried away by his charades, listened inattentively to his literary judgements and, especially – those who got lost in contemplation of the Princess. Unfortunately, Radetsky was a living combination of all these qualities and shortcomings. Vladimir Lukianovich pondered deeply; any outing alarmed him; and this uninvited guest alarmed him. Foreseeing trouble in advance, he began, as we have seen, at his leisure and very subtly, to make fun of him, naturally enough not to his face. From the side, he would start speaking about the then newly appearing Romantic school, which served journalists as a target for their blank cartridges, just as now do sincerity, nobility, disinterestedness and so on and so forth.

In that happy time, even journalists concerned themselves only with literature; nowadays they have come to their senses – literature is the last thing they care about. Vladimir Lukianovich often talked just about arrogance, about young men's vanity, about their bad taste.

'It is well known that the most banal thoughts can be the most lofty ones and, the other way round, the most lofty are the most banal – just as the funniest witticism is always the rudest. It all depends on the point of view from which they are presented and who is doing the presenting. When Byron talks of a hatred for life, of his scorn for people, his words are striking. The very same words are absurd on the lips of some journal rhymester. It is not possible to read a book by Silvio Pellico[22] without getting a special feeling, yet every line in it will have been said twenty thousand times before. These, what would seem to be such simple, ideas, which have entered, so to speak, into our own everyday life, can equally and unwittingly occur among his lofty reveries to a genius; and they can also be employed by someone in repetition of what has been heard, without any awareness. What higher thought can there be than that contained in these words, "For the sake of truth, I am ready to sacrifice my life"? And what can be more ridiculous than this pronouncement when it is met with in our journalistic scribblings on social comment...?

'This whole lengthy discussion was essential, in order to explain to you the means by which Vladimir Lukianovich made such a strong impression upon Princess Zinaida. All of his conversation consisted of similar phrases, but to the Princess these were the expression of a sincere and deep inner feeling. And when, from such phrases, Vladimir Lukianovich passed to the appraisal of people who for some reason seemed to him different, how petty, how worthless these people seemed to be to Princess Zinaida, in comparison with the object of her adoration! Radetsky's conversation with the Princess strongly affected Vladimir Lukianovich. Not the slightest flicker was visible on his face; but he had to pay several fines, something which never happened with him, and no wonder – he was listening intently towards the area in which a number of young people were sitting. Only a few words reached his ears, but just from these he was able to judge that what was going on was no joke. In order to break up this conversation, he resorted to the manoeuvre described by Radetsky, which, from one point of view, succeeded completely. Radetsky's final words, through which he had inadvertently alluded to her personal situation, had a strong effect on the Princess. In her ears, incessantly rang the words: *forbidden passion*, and *violation of duty*. She ran off to her room in utter despair. This was not hidden from the perspicacious diplomat; but he saw only the Princess' agitation and, not being able to grasp in full the reasons for this, ascribed the developing disposition to Radetsky. From this moment, Vladimir Lukianovich outlined provisionally to himself a full plan of attack: the first thing was to remove the dangerous rival; and, secondly, himself to take decisive measures. First of all, he needed to satisfy himself as to what degree Radetsky could prove a hindrance to him. The next day, Vladimir Lukianovich left his wife at a ball on a pretext of having business, returned home, and went straight in to Zinaida's room. Zinaida, having sent the wet-nurse off to have her supper, remained alone with Pashenka in her arms…

'You can just imagine the rather small room, the dark blue wallpaper, the carpets; in a corner is a smallish Turkish divan, a small open cupboard with books, a piano, and flowers on the window sills and around the walls. It is dark in the room; in the dim light of the lamp only the divan is lit up. On the divan is a beautiful girl in her white blouse, in that same captivating female outfit (which was only just coming into fashion and which ladies then only dared to wear at home). A rather dark-coloured ribbon encompasses her slim waist; dark glossy hair tumbles loose over her shoulders in fine curls; on her shapely feet are velvet slippers, turned down with fur. The Princess is holding an infant in her arms, who smiles at her and grabs at the curls around her gleaming earrings. The Princess replies with her own smile, playing with her, but dark thoughts are reflected in her pensive look. Her smile is a bitter one; her lively chatter to the child is still doleful; she bends over to her and kisses her, as though to instil into herself an air of innocence and calm – but in vain. Her whole life is revolving before her; she remembers her childhood games and the first impressions made on her by her first furtive readings of poetry: these she recalls word for word. She remembers how her heart thrilled on reading the first novel to fall into her hands, how genuinely she wept over the fate of the heroine, and how she hid the precious and forbidden book under the bed-head, so as to read it through again, with renewed delight. Then it came to her how unresponsively the range of her thoughts had been broadened by reading, how her mind had hardened and her heart stiffened. New, unexpected thoughts from the depths of her soul, as though from another secret world, arose before her. She sensed in herself the origination of new feelings that were involuntarily intermingling in her whole existence and directing a magic light on to everything surrounding her. But then, as so often, having taken such notice of her inner spiritual impulses, she could not recognise herself and was astonished at her regeneration. And then, mockingly, she would look back at herself in the past, compare herself with her peers, and in her heart there would come into being a powerful pride – that human strength and sickness. And so there forms in her an impatience to get out of the tight circle in which her home life has enclosed her. She dreams of being a wife, a mother, she wants to live and to go into action. Ringing ceaselessly in her head are the lines of Salis[23] – so felicitously rendered by one Russian poet,

Act! The wise will be known by their action:
Close behind come immortality and fame.
Act! Signal by your works of passion
To the swift flight of greedy time.

'And so all her reveries, all her senses flow into one definite goal. Before her there arises in reality a prospect of fulfilling all her ideals: a fine man, who is modest, quiet and good. In his discourse she hears those intimate and cherished words which until now she has met only in books, which were answered in her heart, and were unintelligible to all those surrounding her. And this represents a combination of all perfections – in the first man she has really met; and with his appearance come first love, first hopes, and first torments… And this man is right beside her; she sees him every day – but an awful, eternal chasm divides them! She conceals before him her mental storms. When her heart is full to the brim, her head is on fire and her breast is bursting upwards, she escapes him, she doesn't dare touch him, doesn't dare say to him an out of place tender word; she cannot, she must not, love him! And that's how her whole life will pass, an incomplete and false life, like the life of a brilliant insect, nailed to a tree by some cold observer: in vain does it stretch its iridescent wings, it quivers and tears apart. All around is the sun and the free, scented air, and within a long and exhausting pain, without any strength to break away. Neither is there an end to the sufferings of this poor young woman. Whatever might happen, whatever may be the conflux of circumstances, whichever upheavals might shake society, or the whole world – the chasm between the two of them would remain eternal, and before her still stretched a long, long lifetime!

'Will her strength suffice to endure this unbroken suffering? Will she have enough strength to be together with him every day and conceal this struggle with herself, when it so often reduces her to the verge of madness? Will she retain the strength to escape to her room whenever, at a single glance from him, her blood is beating in her veins like a boiling spring, when all thoughts of duty, honour and shame fly from her head as though by enchantment – and she is ready to fling herself into his embraces? "No," thinks the Princess, "it is time to put an end to this; I must leave this house. Mother will forgive me; God will preserve Lydia and her child… a cell in a distant convent, a hair shirt and a rock in the bed-head – this is the only way of saving myself from myself!" But at this moment the infant, as though comprehending her thoughts, grabbed her round the neck with her little hands. The Princess recovered her senses; she again recollected this child's mother and the last words of her own mother, and all her thoughts got mixed up. Her spirit had come to that dreadful and severe state when two opposing duties are fighting it out, when one idea is destroying another, when a person can accuse the self both of egoism and of an irresponsible selflessness. This is when someone painstakingly fingers every twist of the heart, fears self-deception, seeks out the first remote reason for every feeling and for every thought, weighs every impulse, and, in their state of despair, finds no answer…

‘At that moment, the door opened and Gorodkov walked in. He stopped by the threshold, struck by the splendid picture in front of his eyes. The Princess at first didn’t take note of him, but unwittingly shuddered. I don’t know what was going through his mind at that minute, but he was lost in thought. He quietly, almost in a whisper, greeted the Princess and with a deep reticence flung himself into an armchair standing close to the divan. Several minutes passed like that.

“What’s the matter?” the Princess finally asked him with some concern. “Why are you so lost in thought?”

“What does it matter, what I have to think about!” he replied sadly, “there can be lots of things in one’s heart of the sort that one doesn’t discuss, and that inspire an involuntary melancholy.”

“But, they say, telling the tale of one’s preoccupations can ease the pain.”

Gorodkov winced.

“Yes,” he replied, “if people are happy, just like, for example, our young romantic, who has for everything ready phrases and who, to mention just in passing, seems to be making eyes at you – probably in order for a pretext to compose some lacklustre elegy in fashionable taste.”

The Princess flinched. Gorodkov looked at her attentively.

“I don’t think that, from my words, he could compose any superfluous elegy,” she said, with a smile; “I always impart to him enough sharp truths, I should suppose, as to beat out of him any desire to jabber on about his romantic sufferings.”

Gorodkov winced once more; but this time, seemingly, from pleasure, though this was impossible to guess from his face.

“Why worry about him, anyway!” the Princess continued. “It would be better if you told me – what’s wrong with you?”

Gorodkov moved up his armchair.

"I am going to speak openly to you," he said, leaning on the table with his fine, white, aristocratic hands. "What do you think my life is? With whom can I share my heart? What awaits me in the future? You know your sister; you know ...," he added, stumbling somewhat, "she is not capable of understanding me, she cannot be my helpmate in life, nor my friend in adversity, nor a true mother to our children, nor even mistress of the house. It's so good that you are here; out of love for her, you have taken on all her responsibilities. But, you could go and get married, and I could get ill, and die – what would happen to my child then?"

The Princess began to tremble, wanting to say something, but she just clenched her teeth. Gorodkov didn't take his eyes off her.

"Just look how peacefully Pashenka has fallen asleep in your arms. She knows you better than she does Lydia, and, to all intents and purposes, you are her real mother; you are my only friend."

Gorodkov covered his face with his hands but, probably, not tightly enough to be unable to see how the Princess was reacting. – "But, how long can this be for? You will get married; then you will have your own responsibilities, another kind of attachment, your own children..."

"Never!" cried the Princess, beside herself.

He took her by the hand. Zinaida was as though on fire. Incoherent words escaped her lips and froze.

"How can that be?" replied Gorodkov, looking tenderly at her. "You really won't be able to answer for yourself; and, on my part, it would be too shameless to demand such a sacrifice from you. Isn't that right?"

The Princess was in a very disturbed state. Gorodkov again took her by the hand, and kissed it. The unfortunate girl involuntarily pressed herself against his cheek. Her thick curls spilled down their contiguous faces and it was as though an impenetrable shroud covered what was happening at that minute. But the child, awakened by this movement, cried out; and the Princess collected herself.

"It's Pasha's bedtime," she said, got up hurriedly and carried the infant off to the nursery. Gorodkov followed her meditatively. The Princess leaned over the cradle, speaking quickly, in jerky disconnected words. It was as though she was completely in a fever: her face was burning and her hands shaking. At that moment, Lydia appeared in her ball gown, humming a mazurka and all but dancing. She noticed nothing, although the Princess was looking at her like a criminal.

"Pasha isn't well," said her husband, "your sister and I had some difficulty calming her down."

"What is it?" said Lydia, with the dumbfounded stare, which alone served her for the expression of every possible feeling. Taking a look into the cradle, she added:

"She seems to have gone off, and I'm very sleepy now, too; I feel so tired!"

The child in fact had gone to sleep quietly, as she wasn't at all ill. Gorodkov's words had been a lie, but Zinaida had joined in by her silence. Between her and Lydia's husband, a clandestine agreement had already been concluded; she had already felt a necessity to keep something from her own sister… Lydia absent-mindedly imparted her blessing to Pasha, a thing that she never forgot to do and which, apparently, discharged the entire limit of her maternal duty, and made off to her bedroom. Zinaida spent the whole night praying before images and, towards daybreak, almost delirious, she threw herself into bed.

'On the days which followed, Gorodkov's visits became more frequent than previously. Sometimes he said things to the

Princess, which she couldn't fathom; sometimes he simply looked at her, but with the sort of eyes that said more than words. The struggle within the Princess' heart reached its highest level. She dared not even look at her sister, although Lydia understood nothing of what was going on around her, being only too pleased that her husband didn't prevent her from going out and about. The Princess passed nights without sleep and, when she did drift off, then her fevered imagination repeated all the words said to her during the day, all the impulses of her heart, and filled in all that hadn't been said, enticing her into a world of captivating and voluptuous visions. Awakening, she recalled with horror and with delight her nocturnal reveries; she could see herself standing at the edge of an abyss, and she didn't have the strength to stop. Her room, in which everything reminded her of that seductive evening, became unbearable, and her bed – just terrible: she lost the capacity for praying in this room.

'One evening, sitting by her wide open window, with the warm summer breeze treacherously irritating her imagination, the ringing of the church bells could be heard – and a thousand recollections revived within her. She remembered her childhood innocence; and her childish, pure, serene praying. How she really wanted again to awaken these placid feelings in her heart! She almost unwittingly left her room and, herself not knowing how, came to be in the church. And then there occurred the scene described in Radetsky's letter. Her praying put heart into the Princess; the young man's words, so clear and simple, so filled with feeling, affected her; they seemed to her an unexpected help sent down from above. The firmness of her will was now poised to triumph. She decided, with a single blow, to cut the knot of illicit passion, to sacrifice herself, not removing from herself the means of fulfilling her mother's last wish. With heroic determination, she offered the young man her hand. But, after she had written her note to Radetsky, there still remained to her one more difficult thing – to announce her decision to Gorodkov. She chose a moment when husband and wife were together, braced herself, and, in a choking voice, came out with: "I am going to marry Radetsky." Lydia burst out laughing, Gorodkov turned pale, and the Princess hastened to add, "Everything between us is already agreed; our wedding is tomorrow; he is going away from here, so it had to be as soon as…" With these words, her voice broke off… and she left the room. Gorodkov stayed with his wife and uttered a few insignificant phrases, which she scarcely heard, as she was immediately imagining the ball that would have to be given to mark the wedding.

When Lydia had fallen asleep, her husband went off to Zinaida's room, knowing that she would not be able to sleep. The Princess was sitting on the divan; floods of tears were pouring from her eyes.

"I have come to have a word with you about your affairs," said Vladimir Lukianovich with a catch in his throat. "There is not much time left, and there is something I need to settle with you. As your relative, I have to concern myself with something which, perhaps, you yourself have forgotten. We do have an estate…"

The Princess sobbed, "I don't need anything. I am ready to leave everything with you, with your children, and my sister."

"That is not possible. Your husband will find it strange, improper. You will complain about it yourself. You will have new responsibilities… a new attachment… there could be children."

These words, reminding her of that previous, captivating evening, destroyed her most recent firmness; she threw herself on to Gorodkov's neck and in desperation uttered just the one word: "*Vladimir…!*" But through this word duty was forgotten, along with the promise made, and maidenly modesty. The tempter took her in his embraces, and a long, long kiss prevented the Princess from even finishing this word. But suddenly she tore herself from his embrace, rested against the table, and in a trembling voice declared,

"Vladimir! … in God's name, leave me!"

Gorodkov wanted to draw nearer to her, but she folded her arms with a prevailing air, "In God's name, leave me! … Tomorrow, tomorrow you will know everything," she declared, gasping from her tears.

"But tomorrow," Gorodkov replied, "tomorrow you will be married?"

The Princess threw up her hands and covered her face,

"How could you believe that, Vladimir…? Do you really not see..? Do you really not know…? You…alone, there's…only you!" she exclaimed, beside herself, and ran out of the room.

Gorodkov wanted to follow her, but, afraid of waking the domestics, he returned to his own room. Having gone in there, he smiled derisively. "The devil take it!" he said, "this is no laughing matter!" But he glanced in the mirror and took fright at his own image; he glanced back, to make sure there was no one around, and instantly the derisive smile vanished from his face – as though it had never been there. He lay down in his bed and slept really soundly until morning.

On the next day, the Princess wrote her second note to Radetsky. Radetsky replied to this and, on that same day, he left Moscow.

I really don't know what could have happened to the Princess after all this: but, fortunately for her, a particular incident caused a big upheaval in her family life. Lydia, expecting again, had been dancing tirelessly, as I have mentioned already; that very same morning, as Zinaida decided Radetsky's fate, Lydia began to feel unwell. They sent for the doctor; having examined Lydia, he shook his head meaningfully and suggested calling in further doctors for a consultation. However, before the consultation started, Lydia gave premature birth; the doctors declared her to be in a very dangerous state.

The ill state of health of this unfortunate victim of frivolity lasted for a long time. Zinaida didn't leave her bedside. Sometimes the patient would raise herself slightly in her bed and speak in a weak voice, recollecting the days for which balls had been arranged around the city. She would ask for her latest dress to be looked out, one which she had not even found time to try on, and spread out before her on the bed would be ones of silk lace, velvet and satin materials. She would admire these, play with them like a child, and then she would start to cry and order all her dresses to be taken away.

Sometimes, pointing at her husband, she would say to Zinaida, "Please, you be his wife when I die. He's so good… you will be able to please him better than I can. You're such a clever girl; I'm a poor thing, and so stupid!"

But occasionally in these minutes of delirium a fit of jealousy would befall Lydia. "What are you looking at me for?" she would say; "you are just waiting to see how quickly I will die. You are in love with each other… I know… But be careful, Zinaida! He's really so cunning and so nasty; he will deceive you as well… He has all these papers, piles of different papers… he keeps writing… writing…"

Her words would then break off into sobbing or loud laughter.'

'On one occasion in Kazan a small company of government officials was seated at a tea table: all public servants who had been serving for some time, all what would be considered *salt of the earth*. Along with them were several ladies, and among the ladies was our Maria Ivanovna. The conversation was business-like. They were talking about how whoever it was had made his career; much was said in favour of chance, and much in favour of intelligence and initiative.

"No!" said a regimental physician, who liked to play the role of joker, and who, let it be mentioned in passing, tended to flirt quite a bit with Maria Ivanovna, as she very subtly gave me to understand. "No, no," he said, "I found out something recently which was marvellously cunning! The other day, going through my late brother's papers (his brother, a local legal fixer, having died not very long before this), I found a letter from someone, a not inconsiderable official in Moscow, who – I must say – had thought up a most astonishing thing! What do you think of this? He has this sister-in-law, a girl of some means. Their estate has still not been divided up, and the two parts together, evidently, amount to a tidy chunk, and he has really got his paws into this. But this brother-in-law can think and he surmises: what if she, damn her, goes and gets married, and her husband demands half the estate, and to give up any of this wonderful estate would be so vexing! So, what's to be done about it? What do you think could be the answer?"

They all got down to thinking about it.

"Buy it from her for a song!" said an old chamber councillor.

"No, Flor Ignat'ich," replied the physician, "that would be the old way. Now people are cleverer, they've got a bit more subtle! Buy it up for a song, and there'll be rumours; you'll damage your reputation. Nowadays the smart man has various tricks up his sleeve – he can get up to such ruses that – take as long as you like, you'll never guess it. This is what he came up with, gentlemen: he goes up to the sister-in-law with his fine chatter, drives the lass out of her mind, and then repels any suitors from her. Meanwhile, in the indivisible estate, he's moving peasants about, exchanging plots of waste ground, next he'll be setting people free – he's such a fine fellow!"

Maria Ivanovna shuddered and, as she herself said, listening to the physician's tale made her stomach turn; but, while it lasted, she used all her feminine wiles to conceal her emotion.

I don't know what means Maria Ivanovna used to persuade her admirer, but just a few days later a mysterious letter came into her hands and its original was flying off to Moscow, addressed to Princess Zinaida.

Meanwhile, in Moscow, Lydia was weakening with every day. The doctors called her illness wasting consumption, and used other Latin, French and German terms, with the comforting observation that she was incurable.

On one occasion, when Zinaida had gone out into the entrance hall, in order to send off a prescription straight away to the chemist, an unknown man walked in, asking,

"Is this where Princess Zinaida Petrovna lives?"

"And what do you want with her?" asked the Princess.

"I have an assignment," replied the stranger, "to give her a very important letter."

"You may give it to me," said Zinaida.

"I have to hand it her personally."

"Well, I am Princess Zinaida."

She thought that this letter was from some poor supplicant and had no objection to accepting it. She opened it and swiftly skimmed through it – and her legs almost gave way beneath her! Steps could be heard in the next room: she adroitly hid the letter under her kerchief; meanwhile, the stranger had gone away.

That same day, the Princess, pleading a headache, ordered the carriage, to go for a drive. Her face was pale, but calm. Gorodkov ascribed her pallor to the several sleepless nights she had passed, and advised her to look after herself. The Princess replied to him with a smile, "I shall try," she said, "to preserve myself for you." She put particular emphasis on the last word. Gorodkov softly kissed her hand. The Princess settled herself into the carriage and set off for one of her lady friends.

"You must do me a service," the Princess said to her, – "and it's an important service; order your carriage to be harnessed and take me to our chief of nobility."

The Princess' lady friend could not recover her senses from amazement. Her curiosity was aroused alarmingly, but she couldn't obtain any answers from the Princess. They left Princess Zinaida's carriage in the courtyard and set off themselves, without saying at the gateway where they were going. Arriving at the chief of nobility's house, the Princess left her friend in the reception room and herself, with a non-feminine vigour, marched straight into the study.

"Your excellency!" she said in a firm and somewhat solemn voice, "You have been deputed by the government to defend orphans..."

The chief, taken aback by this unusual tone, smiled and said,

"What's wrong, Princess? Who is it that you are so ardently standing up for?"

"For those," replied Princess Zinaida, "who have no one, apart from me, to stand up for them. Don't laugh, for goodness' sake, and don't be too astonished at what I am going to say! Forget that I am a young woman! At this very moment, just a stone's throw away from us, a crime is being committed, which no law can foresee, nor punish, but which a solid human will can forestall."

The chief was listening to the Princess with a growing amazement.

"What I am going to tell you must remain between ourselves. My sister is dying and she will leave a child. I am asking you to be its legal guardian..."

"Forgive me," answered the chief, "but the child will still have a father!"

"That man," replied the Princess, in a very agitated state, "deserves the trust neither of a government, nor of any honest people."

The chief was dumbfounded by this remark; collecting himself, he replied,

"Excuse me, though, Princess! You are rather overdoing it by what you say. But even if I were to believe you, even then, according to law, I could only be nominated accessory to Vladimir Lukianovich, and even that, only with the agreement of the mother."

"The agreement of the mother?" repeated the Princess, with some anxiety. "You, being an honourable man, must help me in that, too. What would be necessary for that?"

"It would be necessary that she should nominate me, in her last will and testament, as accessory to her husband."

"Then you must drive over to see her, together with me."

"Pardon me, but you are far closer for such a purpose."

"I cannot do it. She wouldn't believe me. And I would add that you must talk to her, together with her confessor, and make sure that it's in the absence of her husband."

"You must admit, Princess, that you are putting me in the most embarrassing position; you are forcing me to go secretly to see a dying woman, in order to force her to do something that could be displeasing to her husband, an estimable man, respected in the whole city. No, say what you like, Princess, I cannot agree to that."

The Princess was in despair.

"Estimable… respected…," she repeated, "when I'm telling you that he is without honour, without conscience…"

"But where is there any proof of that?" the chief finally said, losing his patience.

"Proof!" exclaimed the Princess. "Proof! I have the proof, and it's incontestable. But, I implore you, give me your word of honour that you will never reveal the secret which I am going to entrust to you."

"I give you my word as a man of honour and of the nobility."

The Princess, for several minutes, was in some perplexity; finally, having gritted her teeth and muttered to herself, "Oh Lord, another sacrifice," she said, "Read this, sir!""

Gorodkov's letter to the late legal fixer *of Kazan:*

Dear Sir, and most respected colleague, Foma Ivanovich!

I am most highly and warmly obliged to you for fulfilling all my commissions, you have most sincerely shown your longstanding friendship and good will. Your favourable disposition towards me encourages me to request you, firstly, to read through this letter well away from anyone else, for I am disclosing to you something highly confidential, due to which I am not dispatching this letter through the post, but by a reliable means. I am letting you know from the outset that, in the course of these matters, I have to explain my position to you in detail, but that this matter is a very delicate one. That is why, in future letters, I shall not be resorting to explanations, which may not always be convenient, and therefore it is from this letter, my most respected friend, that you must understand what subsequently I shall only be hinting at.

More than once already I have turned to you, my respected colleague and old messmate, to hurry along completion of the sale of forests near the village of Anisovka.[24] You write to me that, despite my agreement, you have held up the sale because you consider the price too low, and fear that I should have had second thoughts. I am extremely grateful to you for such a sign of good will, but my circumstances do not permit me to wait for other buyers. I feel compelled to explain to you quite frankly, on condition obviously that this should remain a matter of complete confidence, not to be entrusted to anyone. My outlining of these circumstances will convince you, my most estimable friend, how essential it is to speed things up, for this is what might have been called a bold-faced opportunity, which will immediately slip from the fingers.

You know, my dear chap, that I personally have neither house nor home behind me. In order to improve my situation and make a career for myself, I, as will not be unknown to you, took a long time finding myself a suitable bride; eventually, the good Lord sent me a wife – a stupid one, it is true, but one of some means, as you will also know. For the moment, my position is not bad, and I am on the right road, both regarding contacts and relatives and, thank the Lord, I am able to be of use not only to myself, but to my friends. But, my most obliging friend, just look thoroughly into my position. You know the expression, 'nothing in this world is to be relied upon'; the future must be borne in mind; should my wife die – God forbid! – once again, if I may put it this way, I should remain a church mouse down and out! It's true that we do have a child, but the child as well – though God forbid! – could die; but even if the child lives, I should still be nothing more than at the mercy of its generosity. That would still be nothing, just a guardianship, my dear fellow...! I know that, even then, I could make ends meet, but it would be totally onerous, and dangerous... what I want is my own means, separate, independent... you understand me, my most obliging friend! For this reason I want, as far as possible, to hurry through the sale of that forest land, albeit for a song, if only not to let slip this opportunity when cash is on offer: as you know, ready cash is something sacred! And by the way, I should add appreciatively, I don't see why I should overlook the other side of the estate either, which the merciful heavens have so opportunely sent me, all the more so as both halves together make a real entity, but separately lose value enormously. Here we have a matter, my dear chap, I repeat, for secrecy, so to speak, of a highly delicate relationship. Please appreciate that my sister-in-law could marry – you understand...? It happens that, if I may say so, she all but clings round my neck. I, of course, being a noble fellow, do not attempt to take advantage of her failings; but, on the other hand, looking at all these circumstances from a serious viewpoint, I find that this conforms extremely well with my intentions. And, there again, it does cross my mind that, all the same, I cannot be her husband; but, at the right moment, I could just turn into some sort of a fancy man – and then, as you will quite see, there would be trouble, and that's all! It is really essential that I should take advantage of this present time, while I still hold in my hands the power of attorney from both sisters for the indivisible management of the joint estate. In all respects, I need to be getting a move on. Either way, it's dangerous for me – whether my sister-in-law gets married, or she doesn't get married: none of us are beyond temptation. There's no telling what could happen! I recoil from shame, people's tittle-tattle. You know that I am a man of nobility and ambition; I don't want to leave myself exposed to any thorns in my side; that's how I prize my reputation.

I am writing all these things to you as to a friend, and I ask you most humbly, upon reading this letter, to destroy it, and in your own letters to me not to mention my circumstances, other than in a highly allegorical manner. Do try, esteemed fellow, immediately upon completion of the act of purchase for the forest to furnish me straight away with a certificate for the security of the whole estate, concerning which I have already written to you. For goodness' sake, do hurry it up, as much as possible; and don't worry about the costs, so long as any delays are prevented. Before taking up the certificates, ask Klementii Fedorov whether he wants to redeem them, or not; if he does want to, then send me the money immediately; otherwise I shall have to take my own measures.

So, farewell, my esteemed fellow! Don't delay in your reply. Forgive me for burdening you with my commissions; but what else can I do, my dear chap? Living is what counts – to the living. I am a noble and a moral sort of fellow: I have never been out for my own gain, even being without monetary subsistence, or in a position to resort to illicit means. But, on the other hand, it would be incredibly stupid not to take advantage of those prospects that now present themselves. I repeat again my request for the destruction of this letter. Finishing with all this, I have the honour of being most respectfully yours, with complete devotion, your sincere friend and humble servant,

V. Gorodkov

'While this letter was being read by the chief of nobility, Princess Zinaida did not remove her eyes from him. She knew the letter by heart; she followed him through every word. She observed the blush which appeared on the face of this man whom she hardly knew, saw his half smile, when his eyes got to the place referring to the Princess – she saw all of that. All that she endured, and by how many years she aged, in those few short minutes, there is no need to relate.

Finishing the letter, the chief said,

"Now I can agree with everything you said; I am at your disposal."

On that same day, the minute Gorodkov was out of the house, the chief, along with a priest and two witnesses, was in Lydia's room. She signed a will, by the terms of which the chief was appointed executor and trustee in accessory to Vladimir Lukianovich, with progeny, moreover, entrusted to the particular care of Princess Zinaida. When all had been completed and all those who had been in the dying woman's room had departed, Vladimir Lukianovich returned. The chief, meeting him in the doorway, bowed coldly and said that he would expect to lose no time in having official dealings with him as his wife's executor. Vladimir Lukianovich already knew of an excursion by Zinaida on the previous day; now the mystery was solved, but only in part. Anxious and enraged, he rushed off to Zinaida's room, but stopped at the door and, putting on a tender and sorrowful air, stepped quietly in.

"What does this mean, Princess? You do not trust me?" – he said, fixing upon her eyes, and knowing their magnetic effect.

For the first, and probably the last, time a malicious smile appeared on the Princess' lips. She looked at her gallant with disdain and threw into his face his letter to the Kazan fixer...

Gorodkov's position was a tricky one. Prudence dictated that he should immediately run in to the sick woman's room, have it out with her, and replace the existing will with a new one – but already Lydia was unconscious. Another few minutes – and she would be no more. A person's demise involuntarily affects the most callous heart. At that moment, he who survives looks at those around, searching in their eyes for some conviction regarding life... Gorodkov found only the cold, reproachful gaze of Zinaida.

The days of the funeral arrangements went by. In the house, everything was washed and swept out and filled again with tobacco smoke. The pharmaceutical vials were thrown out, the furniture put in place, the sun shone on the glassware, and food was being prepared in the kitchen... Gorodkov livened up; at first his groans were to be heard only behind the door; then, at a clearly calculated time, the doors were opened to arriving sympathisers. Vladimir Lukianovich wept and sighed in his official capacity; in passing, he took upon himself an air of outraged innocence and, by means of slight innuendo, painted Princess Zinaida in black colours. Meanwhile, the steward had been sent to her, with a low bow and with notification that the master of the house wished to move in to the rooms she occupied, seeing that, he said, it was very hard for him to remain in those in which the late Lydia Petrovna had lived.

Zinaida left the house, moving in with one of her lady friends – the Princess having not a kopeck to her name.

Little by little, to those newly arriving to give consolation, it was explained that Princess Zinaida had of late displayed a very nasty disposition. She had been attempting to dominate her ill sister and to swindle out of the deceased various benefactions, to the detriment of husband and children. In this arrogant frame of mind, it was even dangerous to leave her with the child; and so on, and so forth. Such black colours slipped effectively enough on to the touches pre-made.

The time came for the reading of the will. There were two. The first granted Gorodkov unlimited rights over children and estate; the second was the one I spoke of above. It alone, as the last will, had any legal force.

Gorodkov, having listened to all this, coldly declared,

"I am very pleased that I have, in the respected Ivan Gavrilovich [such was the chief's name] such a worthy accessory; but I consider it my duty to state that the deceased was a debtor to me for a sum that exceeds the worth of the estate. If greater trust had been shown in me, a father [and this was said through tears], and there hadn't been any exterior interference, I would have torn up the acknowledgements of debt – after all, what are they to me? Am I really not my child's father? But now I consider myself duty-bound to present them, in order to preserve my child's property from exterior jurisdiction."

All of these words were pronounced in a tone that was dignified, noble and touching. They produced a visible effect on all the listeners: many of them cried, and others spoke with disapproval of the intriguer, Zinaida.

She alone did not lose her head.

"That's not true!" she exclaimed, when the chief all but accused her of having made a complete fool of him. "It's not true! My sister could not have been in debt to him – he had nothing to give her. I shall demonstrate before a judge the worthlessness of these acknowledgements of debt."

"What, Princess! Will you, a young lady, enter into a lawsuit with your sister's husband?"

"Well, you will present a legal application…"

"That's easily said. What proofs will I be able to produce regarding the worthlessness of these acknowledgements of debt? Do you know what this will lead to? Gorodkov would need to be indicted with dishonourable behaviour…"

"And do you still doubt this, after that letter of his?"

"Yes, the letter! Would that letter really serve your interests? Just think about it: it does compromise you…"

"Whatever may be necessary!" she replied, but then, thinking again, she asked with a quiver, – "Is the letter essential?"

"Essential."

"Gorodkov has it!"

The trustee's arms went limp. He absolutely rejected any lawsuit.

The Princess was in despair, but she didn't lose her spirit. Without money and without friends, afflicted with society's chatter, the disapproval of honest, but deceived, people – she embarked on a lawsuit over the non-validity of the acknowledgements of debt assigned by her sister. In support of such an action, she was forced into revealing Gorodkov's liaison with a certain immoral woman who, having outwitted Vladimir Lukianovich himself, was extracting money from him and, in all probability, was needing to get him into marriage with her. The necessity of possessing capital for such a lawsuit forced the Princess to institute another one, for the division of the estate, and then add to this process a third one, dealing with Gorodkov's ruining of the estate. And in all the drawing rooms and workplaces, everyone talked about, laughed about and censured the young woman who had forgotten shame, surrounded herself with shyster lawyers and officials. Garrulity and slander added to all this thousands of insulting misrepresentations, which presented some sort of an air of truth.

Amid the very height of all this business, there returned to Moscow from Paris the uncle of the two sisters, Prince Z... The Princess threw herself at him, as at her deliverer. She told him the whole story, telling him with ardour, feeling and strength. The old prince, prim and proper, in brown tails with a foreign star, at first understood nothing; but the ardour with which his niece spoke somehow got through to his generous soul. He himself suddenly got aroused and he kept saying,

'Comment donc! Nous lui ferons rendre, gorge mordicus!'[25]

One friend of mine once made a very thoughtful comment, to wit: there are some people who are very clever when they speak in French, but who become unbelievably banal and stupid as soon as they start speaking in Russian. This may seem rather strange, but it is correct and natural enough. We learn not the language, but we just acquire by heart thousands of phrases said by clever people in this language. To speak well in French – just means repeating these thousands of ready phrases; these phrases both confuse their ideas and save one from having any of one's own. You listen, a foreign mind emerges from the chatter and misleads you: it seems to be something, but translate it into Russian and it's hogwash – neither here nor there. The prince belonged to that category of people. Hardly had he rolled into anyone's drawing room, when reprimands concerning Zinaida rained down on him from all sides; the good prince was stupefied. Hardly had he started speaking in Russian with business or legal people, when he got completely flustered. Only one thing stayed in his head: that his niece was playing the most ridiculous, the most unseemly role – *un rôle ridicule et peu convenable!*[26]

The prince considered it his duty to put on an air befitting the older relative and, having crossed one leg over the other, to deliver to the Princess the necessary rescuing advice in his purest Parisian speech, complete with cherished sayings and that particular intonation, so unbearably tedious even in the conversation of the native French.

Although he spoke with the Princess in French, and accordingly very intelligently, still he did not convince her. She continued what she had started and there now appeared in the drawing rooms her new persecutor – her own uncle. He would shrug his shoulders, of a morning assuring one and all that he was washing his hands of this whole business and, of an evening, with a sigh, driving out to his French vaudeville.

One day, Princess Zinaida's lawyer came to see her.

"Your ladyship," he said, "there now remains just one thing that you can do: *the oath of purification* – and I consider it my duty to notify you that your opponent, saying that for his children a father must resolve himself to anything, is not averse to such an oath."

"But what is an oath of purification?"

"You will have to go with some ceremony to church, and publicly swear to the truth of your deposition regarding the non-validity of the letters of acknowledgement of debt…"

The Princess turned to stone at such tidings. This seemed too much!

But her resolve did not leave her. She was ready even to undertake this self-sacrifice to her beloved child, but she was saved by one of those unexpected occurrences which may be improbable, but which can very simply resolve, by the will of Providence, even the most difficult of problems. Gorodkov was trampled down by horses – and he died. At his last gasp, he either didn't wish, or didn't manage, to ask for Zinaida's forgiveness.

The death of Gorodkov returned to the unhappy young woman all rights over her niece. She took her in, refrained from getting married, and every minute of her life she dedicated to the child's upbringing. And in the drawing rooms the talk was that she, having thrown her family into disorder, had now put on a mask and was playing the role of the affectionate relative, so as to cover over her old sins and, at the same time, profit from her niece's estate.'

'All this is what I learned,' my friend continued, 'from Maria Ivanovna. Of course, she told me all this in much shorter form than I have been telling it to you. But you are an exact person – you would need to know all the details. This story awakened in me a powerful curiosity to make the acquaintance of this unusual woman, who, in her small family circle, had managed to show more nobility and steadfastness than many men do in much higher fields of life.

Countess Darfeld hosted masked balls on a Tuesday. That winter, the masked ball was all the rage. Everyone dressed up, mystified each other, danced and ran after one another for all they were worth. All the captivating charms of the old-fashioned Italian masquerade were relocated under the northern snows.

One evening I was watching with fascination the variegated world revolving around me. I was almost at the end of my tether with annoyance at the masks, which allowed me no relaxation. "Princess Zizi is here," someone said behind me. "Where, where?" asked someone else. "There she is, sitting in the green domino; my niece is with her."

This brief conversation was quite enough for me. I made off towards the green domino... I had never in my life seen such a shapely waste, such beautiful legs – which, you know, are for me almost everything in a woman. From under her cowl could be seen the black, fine curls that I had heard much about, and through the openings in the mask shone her vivacious, gleaming eyes.

"Please allow me to mystify you," I said, although I was not wearing a mask.

I sat down beside the Princess and suddenly began to relate to her the whole of her story, in all its details. The Princess was alarmed at my narrative; but my sympathy for her, and the respect for her exploit, which my every word exuded, touched her. When I had finished, she said to me:

"Thank you. You have given me my greatest satisfaction in life: to see that slander has not managed entirely to blacken me and that there are people convinced of the purity of my heart."

On the following Tuesday we met, as good acquaintances already. The Princess' conversation was lively, intelligent and entertaining. I didn't notice the hours pass, or the way we were being looked at by the curious.

On the third Tuesday, I considered it necessary also to dress in a domino, so as to be able to converse more comfortably with the Princess.

What can I tell you about it! Within a short time, being with the Princess for me became essential. In vain did I look for her in the drawing rooms; she went out only to masquerades. Without a domino she was afraid to show herself off in society and wanted to accustom herself to it all over again only beneath her mask.

Eventually, at the end of a long evening, which I consider one of the happiest in my life, going out through the entrance, I said to her,

"Princess! I find it hard seeing you only once a week; please allow me to call in on you."

She thought for a bit and then replied,

"That's not possible!"

"But why ever not?"

"I live virtually alone. You know what Moscow is like, and you know what they would start saying, were you to be calling on me."

These words made me, in my turn, stop and think.

"Listen," I said, "don't consider me to be frivolous, or thoughtless. What is such talk to you? Are there really not ways of making fun of any slanderers?"

"Oh, is that so?" – she asked, almost mockingly.

This mockery vexed me. I kept talking and talking, and I don't know myself how I came to tell her that I was madly in love with her, and to offer her my hand.

The Princess gave a deep sigh.

"And I am very fond of you, young man," she replied, "but you know very well that such a thing has to be thought over…"

At this point the carriage reserved in her name was announced with a shout, and the Princess hurriedly left me, saying,

"Until next Tuesday! Before that, I forbid you to come calling on me…"

That night I went through every gradation of the madness of love. I would be writing letters, throwing myself into my armchair, covering my face in my hands, and wandering from corner to corner – as well as… oh, how would you ever list it all?

By morning I had no strength left. I jumped into my carriage and gave the order to be driven to Princess Zinaida. She made me wait quite a long time by the doorway, but finally I was received. I ran up the staircase like one possessed and the first object that struck my eyes in the drawing room was the Princess – dressed in her domino.

"You did not obey my request," she said, "– what are we going to do with you? I want to punish you for that, so you will be allowed to speak with me, but not to see me…"

I rushed over to her and started imploring her to take off her mask. What exactly I babbled, I don't remember, as I was in a complete frenzy.

"Let's sit down," she said to me, "and talk; it's a serious matter… You love me, young man. I believe you; I trust your pure, young and fair soul. When I look at you, the thought occurs to me that I could still be happy in life… yes, my good sir, I am almost not indifferent to you… you have revived for me the old, forgotten feelings… how I would like to prolong this moment…"

I was beside myself. I kissed her hand and my breath caught.

"Wait a minute!" said the Princess, "there is one obstacle in this matter, and it's a very important one…"

"An obstacle!" I said, " – what is it? After all, you are free."

"Not a very big obstacle, but an important one," the Princess repeated, with a laugh, removing from her face her mask, "– I am forty, and you are barely eighteen! My niece is the same age as you, and she's already married! It's a shame to frustrate your enchantment, and my own, but you are too late, and so am I. I am not fated to have this kind of happiness in life – and, as for you, you will find another kind."'

'What is there to tell you further!' – my friend went on. 'I started trying to think up trite phrases about just being young in the face, about the age difference not preventing happiness, and so on and so forth; but my words somehow didn't come off, and the Princess seemed sadly and sardonically amused at my discomfiture. The next day I left Moscow. But anyway, it's time I went off to the exchange.'

He picked up his hat.

'Hang on! Wait a minute!' I shouted after him. 'How was it that you didn't guess the Princess' age from all these letters?'

'Didn't I tell you? I only got hold of those after the conclusion of this whole story,' was my friend's reply.

NOTE ON RUSSIAN PRINCELY TITLES

The pre-revolutionary Russian title of 'Prince' (*kniaz'*) was held and inherited by the members of the old families that traced their descent from Rurik, the viking (Varangian) leader who founded Russia, or *Rus'*, in the ninth century). Odoevsky was himself the last member of such a family (and in his later years ranked as 'Russia's premier nobleman'). The Romanovs , who were awarded the throne in 1613, had previously been just one of these families. Imperial princes bore the title *velikii kniaz'* (anglicised to 'Grand Duke' and 'Grand Duchess'). Other hereditary titles, in particular 'Count' (*graf*) were bestowed by the Tsar (or Emperor) – take, for instance, the family of (Count) Leo Tolstoy – or were inherited through some foreign origin (notably the Germanic 'Baron').

Russian (here forgetting the 'Grand Duchess' variety and further diminutive forms) has two words for 'Princess': *kniagínia* and *kniazhná*. The latter is an unmarried daughter of a Prince, and the eponymous Mimi and Zizi both fall into this category. *Kniagínia*, on the other hand, is the wife of a Prince (for example, Mimi's mother). As English has just one word, clarity in the translation has occasionally been preserved by employing the epithet 'old Princess' (though in some cases the adjective was present in the original anyway).

NOTES

1. Caesar's wife must be above suspicion. (French)
2. Keep your shoulders back! (French)
3. 'One chats, one laughs, one is happy.' French novels
4. Alexander Griboedov (1795–1829), dramatist, poet and diplomat; plus characters from his play *Gore ot uma* (*Woe from Wit*)
5. Romantic drama (1831) by Alexandre Dumas, *père*
6. Pierre de Bourdeilles de Brantôme (1540?–1614), French memoirist
7. Vasily Vasilevich Tredyakovsky (1703–69), Russian poet, translator and literary theorist; his translation of Tallemant's *Voyage de L'Isle d'Amour* (1663) appeared in 1730.
8. 'If you want to make me cry…' (French)
9. Johann Caspar Lavater (1741–1801), Swiss writer and pastor, chiefly remembered for his writings on physiognomy
10. Being true to the spirit of one's age! (French)
11. Theatrical term for a leading man (French)
12. Madame de Genlis, or Stéphanie, Comtesse de Genlis (1746–1830), French writer and educator (who had published her memoirs in 1825)
13. How are you? (French)
14. The future does not belong to anyone, Sire, the future is in God's hands. Victor Hugo (1802–85)
15. 'You are going to harp on to me about goodness knows what common morals, that are on everyone's lips, ringing out loud and clear, as long as no one is obliged to practise them. / But if they rush into crime? / That's up to them.' (French) *Rameau's Nephew* (1761?), a novella in dialogue form by Denis Diderot (1713–84)
16. Yekaterina Aleksandrovna (1804–61): a princess by birth, married to a general, she had been friendly with Odoevsky before her marriage.
17. The baron is embarrassed. (French)
18. Griboedov's famous play *Woe from Wit* includes a Princess with six daughters, two of whom are named Mimi and Zizi.
19. Nikolai Karamzin (1766–1826), Russian writer and historian
20. This apparently refers to the contributions to eighteenth-century French travel literature by Joseph Laporte (1718–79).
21. Vasily Andreyevich (1783–1852), prominent Russian Romantic poet and translator (second, in his day, only to Pushkin)
22. Sivio Pellico (1789–1845): Italian political activist and dramatist
23. Johann Gaudenz von Salis-Seewis (1762–1834), Swiss poet-sentimentalist
24. The mutually owned estate of the two sisters
25. Well, now! We'll get it all back from him, the devil take him! (French)
26. A ridiculous and none too decent role. (French)

BIOGRAPHICAL NOTE

Prince Vladimir Fyodorovich Odoevsky (or 'Odoyevsky') (1804–69) was the last member of a princely Russian family that traced its descent from Rurik, the Viking leader who founded Russia in the ninth century. Odoevsky is now mainly remembered as one of the best Russian Romantic and Gothic-Fantastic storytellers, often called 'the Russian Hoffmann'; he was the author of artistic stories, and particularly of the unusual frame-tale philosophical novel, *Russian Nights* (1844). He also, however, had strong social interests, displayed in his anti-utopian stories, but not least in his society tales of the 1830s.

Odoevsky was, though, a man of many talents and careers. He held various posts in government service in St Petersburg, and finally returned to his native Moscow as a Senator. But he was also a musical expert (even inventing his own instrument) and a keen writer of educational works for the peasants (preceding, in this field, Leo Tolstoy). He was also an amateur scientist, directed a big library and a museum, and spent much of the second half of his life on philanthropic work. He wrote children's stories, which remain popular through to this day, and even penned culinary articles, under the name of 'Mister Puff'. He hosted, together with his wife, an influential St Petersburg salon and had close contact with all the main cultural figures of his period, from Pushkin and Glinka to Tolstoy and the young Tchaikovsky.

Neil Cornwell is the author of two monographs on Odoevsky (published in 1986 and 1998) and the translator of Odoevsky's *The Salamander and Other Gothic Tales* (1992). He has also translated Daniil Kharms (*Incidences*, published by Serpent's

Tail, 1993; reprinted 2006) and Vladimir Mayakovsky (*My Discvovery of America*, published by Hesperus in 2005). His other authored books include *The Literary Fantastic* (1990) and *The Absurd in Literature* (2006). He has also edited the *Reference Guide to Russian Literature* (1998) and *The Routledge Companion to Russian Literature* (2001), as well as the collection *The Society Tale in Russian Literature: From Odoevskii to Tolstoi* (1998).

He is now Professor Emeritus (Russian & Comparative Literature) and Senior Research Fellow at the University of Bristol.